The Marquess is Mine

League of Unweddable Gentlemen, Book 6

COPYRIGHT

The Marquess is Mine
League of Unweddable Gentlemen, Book 6

Cover Art by Wicked Smart Designs
Editor Grace Bradley Editing

ISBN: 978-0-6450581-0-9

PLEASE NOTE

The Marquess is Mine was previously part of the Christmas anthology, Have Yourself a Merry Little Secret.

DEDICATION

For everyone who loves a little Christmas romance…

PROLOGUE

St. Albans Abbey, Kent
1815, Summer

"Get off her, you tyrant!"

Young women of a particular age were wont to become romantic. It was no different for Lady Sarah Farley, youngest child of the late Duke of St. Albans, at the impressionable age of fourteen. With those words uttered to her eldest brother, Henry, by her younger brother's best friend, it was the exact moment that she fell in love with the boy.

Lord Giles Longe, Marquess Gordan. Her hero.

Henry stepped back from trying to take Sarah's self-portrait she was finishing. A sketch her father had started and one of the last things he had done with her before he passed the previous year. "This is my house, Gordan, and I can do whatever I want. I'm the duke. You're nothing but a child who should know when to speak to his betters."

Her hero scoffed, pulling Sarah to stand behind him.

"I'll try to remember my manners the next time I'm before one."

Sarah looked between Lord Gordan and Henry and didn't miss the hatred they felt. It was so palatable that she could almost taste it. Lord Gordan, Giles to his friends, was two years younger than her elder brother, the duke, and already at nose level. Her brother's eyes were narrow and unkind, Giles was the opposite, wide and clear and filled with a compassionate light.

Her favorite brother, Hugh, had invited Giles to spend the summer with them, and he had arrived only yesterday. Sarah could not remember having been more excited about having house guests. With her father's passing, they had been in mourning a year, but this summer, her mama had allowed Hugh to invite his school friend. The moment she had spied the devilishly handsome gentleman alighting from his carriage from the attic window, her heart had moved.

For a boy of eighteen years, the same as Hugh, he moved with grace and ability. He was tall but did not look awkward in his frame. Oh no, already his shoulders were wide, strong, and gave a hint to a rakehell in the making.

Every gentleman Sarah thought handsome was destined to turn into a rake. She sighed, glancing down at his hand that remained on her wrist, holding her away from Henry. Such lovely, strong hands too. Perfectly shaped for holding one against one's heart.

In only a few short years, she would be off to London, to have her first Season, and then men like Lord Gordan would court her, flirt, and wish to marry her. As a duke's daughter, she would have ample to choose from. Not that she needed to accept any who bowed before her, for her heart had been moved by Giles and would forever belong to him.

"Are you unharmed?" he asked, leaning down to be closer to her shorter height. Henry told her a duke's daughter did not need a self-portrait. That as duke's daughter, they could hire a painter for such menial work. No sister to a duke should be sketching so.

Henry was a fool.

Sarah was well aware of what was expected of her in society when her time came to enter it. Until then, she would not allow him to take the things that meant more to her than life itself. The drawing her father started being one. Her father would never have allowed Henry to treat her with such disrespect, and neither would Hugh, who stood behind her, glaring at their elder sibling.

"Leave her alone, Henry, or I'll bloody your nose like I did last week."

Henry sneered at the three of them. "I'll cut you off, you two, you'll be left with nothing if you do not do as I say. Now get outside and play like children if that is how you're going to behave, with your stupid sketches and silly school friends who come to stay."

"Gladly," Hugh said, gesturing for Sarah and Giles to join him. "Come on, we'll do as the duke says. Let him have his lofty ideals and solitude, we can have better fun outdoors anyway."

Sarah followed, but not before Henry took one last swipe for her drawing. This time he clutched it, and laughing, ran over to the roaring fire, and threw it onto the flames. Sarah screamed, reaching for the parchment, but Giles grabbed her, hoisting her back from the flames that wrapped about the image and consumed it.

"Sarah, no, you'll hurt yourself."

A sob wrenched up from somewhere deep inside, and she lent a scream. Tears streamed down her cheeks as her sketch darkened and burned before her eyes.

"You bastard." The sound of a fist hitting flesh rent the air, and Sarah turned to see Henry's legs go flying over the settee, his own cries of pain muffling the sound of her sobs. "How could you do that to Sarah?"

Henry stood, his footing a little unsteady as he pinched his bloody nose, trying to stem the bleeding. "Easily, she's a baby and needs to grow up, and mark my words, Hugh, should you hit me again it'll be the last time."

"Touch anything of Sarah's again or her, and it'll be your last day on earth," Hugh said, pulling her into his arms and helping her from the room. Sarah sobbed against her brother's chest, and no matter how they tried to make her happy, distract her with ideas of finishing the fort her father had started to build last year, fishing or swimming, she would not be moved.

Today she needed time to mourn her loss. Her father's drawing. Their drawing. "I think I shall go upstairs to my room. I do not feel like going outdoors just now."

Her brother and Giles walked her to her door and waited as she stepped into her suite, her sanctuary. Hugh walked off, but Giles watched her as she turned to shut and lock the world away.

"I'm so sorry, Sarah."

She shrugged, wiping away more tears as they fell. "Henry has always been a selfish beast. Today he merely proved it before someone outside our family."

Giles reached out, lifting her chin to meet her eye. His thumb slid across her cheek, wiping away the tears that fell unheeded. She hiccupped, the lump in her throat hard to swallow past.

"I do not like to see you cry."

His dark, stormy eyes were filled with concern, and she reached up, touching his hand. "I will be well again, my lord."

Lord Gordan did not look convinced, and yet at her brother's command to join him, he reluctantly stepped back. "When you're ready, join us outdoors. Although the summer has not started off well for you, Hugh and I will make it fun and one to remember."

She nodded, not quite convinced that would be the case, but willing to try. "Of course." She rallied a smile, wanting him to believe she was well again, even if her heart ached for her loss.

"While I'm here, His Grace will not touch you or anything you own."

Her heart gave a decided flip at his words. Hugh's friend was not only handsome, but he was also honorable. He strode off down the hall, and she watched him go, bedazzled a little by his sweetness.

Sarah could not wait to have her first Season. What a pity she had four more years to wait. The thought discouraged her all over again.

CHAPTER 1

St. Albans Abbey
December 20, 1829

There were two things in life that Lady Sarah Farley, sister to the duke of St. Albans disliked more than anything else in the world. Entertaining Marquess Gordan, or Giles as she'd once called him, and seeing Marquess Gordan in her home.

When they had been friends.

The sight of the beast across the ballroom floor where the Christmas house party her brother Hugh and his new wife, Molly, were hosting was not to be borne. Or the fact that he hadn't even gazed in her direction for the past hour.

Beast.

Was she still as invisible as she'd always been with this man? Romantically at least. It hadn't always been so between them, they had been friends once. A long time ago, but no longer. *Ass*, not man, she corrected, sipping her champagne and glaring at him over the rim of her glass.

Why her brother Hugh had invited him in the first place confounded her. She'd begged him not to, had told Molly the reasons why the marquess should not attend. Well, at least the ones she could admit to publicly, and yet, the fiend had arrived and was strutting about the room as if he owned it.

Peacock.

"Please do not be angry with Hugh, my dear. Lord Gordan was an old friend and one he has missed. Having him here will help in clearing your brother's name in the eyes of the *ton*."

"People already know the truth, no point in bringing back the old guard simply to please them more. Hugh has other friends. Lord Gordan does not need to be reimagined into the fold." Sarah wasn't sure she could stomach much more of these so-called friends returning into her brother's life after distancing themselves from him when he needed their support most.

She had never believed her elder brother Henry's claims, or that of her late mother that Hugh had been the one to ruin Miss Laura Cox, an heiress, several years before. Henry had always been selfish, a well-seasoned liar, and someone who could not be trusted. The favored son, eldest and the Duke of St. Albans, it was not surprising that their younger brother was asked to take the fall, the shame that Henry could not face himself.

"You really do not like Lord Gordan do you, my dear? Is there something you wish to tell me? Other than your more benign reasons you have already noted as to why he should not be here?" Molly asked her, taking her hand to make her look at her sister-in-law.

Sarah shook her head, not wishing for anyone to know her shame. Her regret. "No, I merely do not agree with some of these men showing up here and pretending that they are long-lost friends. That Hugh's displacement half a world away was not of their doing. They may have forgotten, but I have not. I missed years of being with Hugh because of this catty society. I will not forgive them."

Molly leaned over and kissed her cheek. "Hugh loves you so very much, and so do I. We do not want you to be unhappy. It is Christmas, after all. Forget about those gentlemen who now scramble about Hugh's feet and look to others for amusement and flirtation. Focus on ones who did not turn their back on your brother. There are many eligible men here for the month-long house party. Surely there are others who may take your fancy."

Sarah sighed, wishing that were the case. It was not. There had only ever been one man whom she'd longed for. Had wanted with such rebellious disregard that she'd acted on that impulse many years before and lived to regret her actions.

How dare the cad even show up here. He ought to be horsewhipped, and by her. This idea was tempting, and if she put on a warm enough cloak, she could fetch a whip from the stables and do exactly what she envisioned.

How had she been so stupid and irresponsible all those years ago? After her brother's banishment from England, one would think one would learn to be careful. To follow the rules society placed upon their young heads and not step out of line.

Not Sarah. She had thrown herself at his lordship during her first Season. As the wealthy daughter of a duke and now a sister to one, she had thought herself invincible. A woman whom any man would gladly fall at her feet and then sweep her off those said feet and marry her.

Lord Gordan had not, and it was not until she had

kissed him on the darkened terrace, practically threw herself against him, pushing him up against the ivy trellis that she realized her mistake.

He'd not kissed her back.

In fact, he'd set her from him, gave her a proper verbal scolding that even to this day made her ears burn, and had stormed back indoors to her elder brother's ball and had barely spoken to her since.

Not that she cared if she ever spoke to the man again. He did not deserve her regard or friendship, even if their icy exchanges were solely due to Sarah's lack of manners.

"I will forget about Lord Gordan and enjoy the house party. I promise I shall enjoy our Christmas together." Sarah smiled as Molly thanked her before rejoining her husband, Hugh. When his wife was close enough, Hugh wrapped an arm about her side and pulled her against him, keeping her close.

Sarah's heart twisted a little in her chest. How lucky Molly was to be loved and adored as much as her brother loved and cherished her. Their love and Molly's trust in Hugh gave her hope that she would one day find a grand love that would make her skin prickle and her body thrum.

Well, she had found that love until he up and proposed to someone else. She spied Lord Gordan coming toward her with determined steps, and she steeled herself for the forthcoming confrontation.

"Lady Sarah, how very festive you look this evening in your red-and-green gown. Anyone would think it was Christmas." His deep baritone made goose bumps rise on her skin, and she cursed his ability to make her not herself, even after all these years, and the time they'd been enemies and not friends.

Sarah bit back a scathing retort, mentioning that his

sarcasm and lack of praise on her gown were not missed. But, because she promised her sister-in-law not minutes before to behave, Sarah smiled up at Lord Gordan and threw him a halfhearted smile. "How very astute you are, my lord. That schooling you partook in at Cambridge really has paid off that you're able to understand my color choices at this time of year."

He raised one brow, his lips thinning into a straight line. Lips that she knew to this day were as soft as butter, and made her feet curl up in her silk slippers. She licked her lips, wondering if hers had been as supple. Possibly not, she was forever chewing them, and she rode her horse a great deal. The air and sunlight did little good for one's skin, when one had too much of them.

"My parents were most proud of my academic record," he quipped, coming to stand at her side. "I have not seen you in town these past few seasons. Have you grown bored with London society? I do miss your impulsive kisses very much," he whispered, leaning down to ensure privacy.

Sarah gaped at his lordship. How dare he bring up her oversight? "It is not the act of a gentleman to bring up the foolish mistakes that a lady may have made in her youth. I have little doubt that my actions that night were brought on by my champagne sampling for the first time."

"Really?" he asked, cocking one brow. "And here I was thinking that your molesting of me was solely due to my charm and good looks. How very disheartening to know the truth."

Sarah ground her teeth, little amused by his teasing of her. "My memory, if correct, was that you did not like my kisses and told me so very abruptly to my face. I see no point in our conversing now." There, that ought to do it. He would leave now, and she could go on brooding, glaring at everyone who now thought her brother a respectable duke when only a year or so ago would not mention his name in polite society.

"We do not have to converse." He threw her a wicked grin, and once more she was lost for words.

Was he flirting with her?

The rogue!

He ought not. It would not get him anywhere. She had long given up any hope she may have had with his lordship. Sarah made a point of trying to find someone in the crowd. "I believe Lady Rackliffe is here this evening. Are you sure you do not wish to commence your love affair with her again? She's a widow now. Maybe this time she'll turn up for your wedding." Sarah chuckled, sipping her mulled wine and enjoying the fact that her words had shut the cocky marquess up.

He took a sip of his whiskey, staring out at the dancers before them. For a country Christmas party, Molly had invited many of their friends. Her closest four friends now congregated about Molly, and they laughed and talked as if they had not seen each other in years and not merely weeks.

Sarah wished she had friends like Molly. She'd been neglected as much as Hugh had been by their mother. However, her father had always been loving, but unfortunately, he passed when she was young. She was so thankful that Hugh was now home in England, although they would be returning to Rome sometime next year. They planned on traveling between their two houses, and Sarah had promised to go with them next year to see Rome and Naples.

"By my calculations, you are eight and twenty, my lady. I thought by now that you would have been married. Why ever have you not? No lord in London good enough for Lady Sarah Farley?"

She glanced at him. How dare he mention her name or turn the question back onto her?

"Spying on me, Lord Gordan? I did not know you were so very observant to my every move."

He scoffed beside her, sipping his whiskey. "You do hold yourself in high esteem. I was merely keeping watch on my friend's sibling while he was out of the country."

"Of course you were, my lord."

A shadow flickered in his eyes before he blinked, and it was gone. Did he remember how very close they once were? That he had been one of her best friends in the world? Or so she understood. All lies, of course. He'd not cared about her at all. Had only ever seen her as Hugh's younger sister and someone to protect, but never love.

Those summers seemed so long ago now. So much had happened between them that there was no way they would ever get back the friendship they lost.

"I hope that I did not teach you to be so cold and aloof as you are. Why, before I came over here to speak to you, you were busy scowling at everyone." He reached out with his thumb and smoothed the frown line between her brows. “What has you so out of sorts, Lady Sarah?”

The moment his skin touched hers, the breath in her lungs hitched. She slapped away his hand, but not before reading the awareness that flared in his eyes. He'd felt it too, the reaction they had always had to each other. Their first kiss was proof of that, no matter what Lord Gordan professed otherwise. She was certain it had affected him as much as her, no matter his anger over the embrace may have said otherwise.

A question lingered in her mind over what would

happen should they act upon those feelings now. Would things progress differently between them? She could have sworn when she'd kissed him all those years ago, for a moment, he'd kissed her back. Having never kissed anyone before, she had never been certain if she had imagined his reaction or not, fleeting as it was.

Her body ached with want for him, for his lips to touch hers. From the age of eighteen, she knew her infatuation with Lord Gordan was more than just a young girl's fancy. She'd wanted him to be hers, and he did not want the same.

He had wanted Lady Rackliffe, Lady Edith Beadle then, an earl's daughter and sweet on Lord Gordan. Or so he believed.

Fool that he was, that had turned out not to be the case.

"Do not touch me, Lord Gordan. You forget yourself."

He bowed, seemingly sorry for his lapse in manners. "Apologies." He looked contrite, as if he had indeed lost his faculties for a moment. "It shall not happen again."

"I should hope not." She sipped her wine, noting that he didn't move away, but kept beside her, quiet and still. "Was there anything else that you wanted from me, my lord?"

A muscle worked in his jaw before he said, "You did not answer my question. Why are you so incensed this evening?"

She ground her teeth, hating that the one man she did not want to know her secret would ask such a question. Truth be told, he made her angry. His denial of her. His pushing her away. His severing their friendship the moment Hugh had left England.

"I'm not angry, my lord, merely weary of a gentleman

like you who believes a woman should always look happy and jovial. I do not need to smile and simper just to please those about me. I'm a daughter of a duke, a sister to one, and have my own inheritance. If I wish to stand at the side of a ballroom and glare at those I do not think worthy of my family's hospitality, I shall do so."

His eyes widened before he glanced back at the dancers. "Are you saying that I'm not welcome here, my lady?"

She shrugged, feigning nonchalance when in truth, her heart beat loud in her chest. Giles had always been welcome at the Abbey, and most of all, by her. To say otherwise now would hurt him, but the slighted, angry debutante inside her growled at his denial of her. The injury he'd caused her heart that had never truly healed. "Hugh is happy for your company, that is enough, is it not?"

He scoffed. "I suppose it will have to do."

Sarah watched him stalk off, anger thrumming across his wide shoulders. A little piece of pleasure rolled through her that she'd hurt his feelings while, in turn, her heart ached at his leaving.

Her eyes met those of her brother across the room, and she smiled, feigning pleasure. He threw her a dubious look that spoke of a future conversation between them over her antics with Lord Gordan. She sighed. A month more of this would be a chore.

CHAPTER 2

Giles stormed from the ballroom and ran directly into the path of Lady Rackliffe. He inwardly groaned at his apparent good luck this evening. First, his run-in with Sarah and now Edith, his ex-betrothed. She stared up at him, all innocent as if butter would not melt in her mouth. A marvel, really, considering she had failed to arrive at church on their wedding day, preferring another over him.

The blonde goddess, Lady Rackliffe, was indeed a muse for men's fantasies. Large, voluptuous breasts, long, golden locks, and cool, blue eyes that slanted a little and gave her a wicked, enticing appearance that had once drawn him like a moth to a candle flame.

Not anymore. Now he looked upon her with the knowledge of what a spiteful, using minx she was.

Sarah floated through his mind, she too had long, blonde locks, but of a warmer hue, as if the sun had kissed her curls. Her eyes were a dark shade of green that he'd often thought the Scottish Highlands would be jealous of.

His body clenched, and he repudiated the idea that

Sarah hated him. He deserved her wrath, just like the woman before him deserved his after she had jilted him, thrown him over for a much older, richer peer.

An ancient relic who had conveniently died within twelve months of their marriage, leaving her an heiress.

"Giles, darling. How wonderful to see you again. We should talk while we're at the house party. It has been too long."

He picked up her hands as they snaked their way up the folds of his jacket to wrap about his neck. He did not want her touching him any more than she had wanted to marry him.

"I would like that, Lady Rackliffe, but tomorrow perhaps. I seek my rest this evening. A long day of travel has wearied me." Not to mention the fact that Sarah's dislike of his attendance here hurt more than he cared to know. He wanted to be friends with her again. To be as close as they once were. Her hurried and spontaneous kissing of him during her first Season seemed to have put paid to their association. He cringed, hating himself for telling her off like a spoiled child.

She had not deserved his retort. He ought to tell her why he'd reacted so. Why he'd pushed her away and told her in no uncertain terms how inappropriate her kiss had been.

"Shall we meet somewhere, Giles? St. Albans Abbey has a beautiful, secluded conservatory, I understand. We may catch up there if you wish. After luncheon?"

He nodded, distracted, and having forgotten Lady Rackliffe was before him. "Of course. Tomorrow. Good evening, my lady."

Giles went to start up the stairs, but she halted him, clutching the lapels of his jacket with more force than he thought her capable of. "Are you not going to kiss me goodbye? Surely we're past such formal goodbyes, are we not?"

Giles recoiled at the idea of kissing her, but leaned down, kissing each of her cheeks.

A clearing of one's throat sounded behind him. He whirled about to see Sarah passing him by, starting up the stairs. She made a *tsk tsk tsk* sound. "Behave, dear guests. There is no mistletoe above you to excuse away your display of affection for one another."

Sarah's words were said lightly, playfully even, but Giles could see the anger and disgust that stared at him through her eyes. Lady Rackliffe appeared immune to Sarah's veiled criticism of their goodnight kiss.

She tittered before him, smiling up at Sarah. "Lady Sarah, so good to see you again. Where have you been for the last few years? We had thought that you ran off to the continent to live with your brother, so long have we not seen you."

Sarah halted halfway up the stairs, turning to meet Edith's amused visage. "If only, my lady. If only," she said, before continuing on and disappearing along the corridor upstairs.

Edith's smile slipped, and Giles bowed, seeing his moment to escape. "If you'll excuse me, Lady Rackliffe. I really must obtain some sleep."

Distantly he heard Sarah's slippered footsteps upstairs. His need to talk to her again paramount. He did not want her thinking there was anything between himself and Lady Rackliffe, as there was not.

"Of course, goodnight, my lord."

"Goodnight." Giles took the stairs two at a time and made his way toward the family apartments in the Abbey.

The building was old, a medieval-like structure more than a modern Georgian home. Still, the Duchess of St. Albans had done a lot to it in the short time she had been married to Hugh, and the house was warm, homey, and once again had a feeling of peace and tranquility he had only ever known it to have when Hugh and Sarah's father was alive.

He turned the corner and spied Sarah almost at her bedroom door. Increasing his pace, he reached her room, just as she went to open it. He clasped the handle, slamming it shut. She spun about, the action placing him hard against her, his breathing ragged.

He swallowed the pleasant feel of her against his chest, her bright-green eyes staring up at him with shock. She blinked, and the contempt was there again, mocking and hating him as it had for years.

"Are you quite done rubbing up against me, Lord Gordan? I should not have to tell you twice in one night to remember who I am."

He stepped back, missing the feel of her the moment he did so. "I needed to explain that what you saw just before was not what it appeared."

Sarah raised her brow. Again, her derisive laugh grated on his nerves. "Really? You do realize, Lord Gordan that I'm eight and twenty and have long learned that when I see gentleman kissing ex-lovers, that one can only assume the ex should be excluded."

"I'm not sleeping with Lady Rackliffe."

She shrugged, her hand reaching behind her to open the door. "I couldn't care less about what you do."

He slammed the door closed again, pressing against her. Of course, he should not, but damn it, she spiked his anger and patience. "Is that true?" He leaned down, taking in the sweet scent of her hair, floral with a hint of rose.

Damn, she smelled as good as she felt in his arms. Her hands fluttered to his chest, the pressure to push him away there, but not forceful.

"Has been for a very long time, my lord. Are you so dense you need me to remind you?"

He flinched, grinding his teeth. A smug look passed over her face, and rage tumbled through his blood. She did not care what he did? Well, he'd test that theory.

Seizing her face in his hands, he leaned down and kissed her.

And he was lost.

CHAPTER 3

The moment Giles's lips touched hers, Sarah knew the horrendous, catastrophic error it was. Not that she did not like having one of the most eligible, attractive, and rich men in all of England kissing her as if his life depended on it, but because a small, traitorous part of her loved it.

Damn him and his mouth that moved over hers, coaxed and teased her senses until her wits were scattered.

For appearance's sake, Sarah pushed at his chest. It was no use. He was steadfast in his preposterous notion of taking her lips and proving his asinine point. Even so, when his tongue slipped across her lips, she sighed, opening to him without realizing the devastation her acquiescence would mean.

He deepened the kiss, and no more was it delicate and beckoning, but hard, demanding. Made that special place between her thighs ache and clench. She pushed her legs together, trying to sate her need. Her hands ran along the lapels of his coat, his breathing ragged, she could feel each breath, the air going into his strong lungs, his chest firm and corded.

He would look so delicious without his clothing. Women had tittered about seeing him just so—the ones who had been fortunate enough to warm his bed. The idea of anyone seeing Giles unclothed so had sent such a shot of jealousy through her that she'd avoided society and all news of him for years, practically becoming a recluse.

That had to change now. With her brother back, the man kissing her to a jelly pool at his feet would be about her often, whether at St. Albans Abbey or town.

Their kiss was madness. Anyone could happen upon them, her family, a servant, her brother! The idea of being forced to marry Lord Gordan was like a cold bucket of water poured over her muddled head, and with all the strength she possessed, Sarah pushed him away.

"Enough," she said, her heart beating fast in her chest. He stumbled back, his eyes heavy and dilated, and she'd seen that look before. He'd looked at Lady Rackliffe so before their engagement.

She ground her teeth, hating that men could be so changeable. "You should not have done that, my lord."

"I have done many things that I regret, but that kiss, Lady Sarah is not one of them."

His words sent heat spearing across her face, and she took a calming breath, hating the fact that after all these years apart, he could still make her blush.

"If you wish to enjoy your time here in Kent, may I suggest that your attention be better spent elsewhere? I am not looking for a husband, nor do I like men who kiss me only minutes after being caught kissing someone else."

He flinched, a muscle working at his temple. "Do be serious. You cannot mean my kiss with Lady Rackliffe."

Sarah raised her brow, staring at him. He shuffled on his feet, glaring at her. "I kissed her cheeks, not her lips, Sarah. If you had seen me," he said, stepping close again, "with my tongue down her throat, there may be a point to your concern." His breath was hot against her ear and she shivered, closing her eyes so as not to see his delectable self.

"It was you that I kissed without heed or caution. I want to kiss you again." His eyes met hers, and she read the longing in them. Her body ached for fulfillment. She was eight and twenty, after all. Like all people, she had needs, and those needs were becoming more and more powerful. Harder to ignore with each year that passed.

Having Lord Gordan tempt her in such a way was unfair, and she knew that she would not get an ounce of sleep tonight.

"Let me kiss you again," he pleaded, his lips brushing hers, but not demanding anything more. "You savored it. Admit it."

"Goodnight, my lord," she said, opening her door and all but throwing herself into her room lest she do exactly as he begged. Her eyes met his as she shut the door, and what she saw there sent heat and expectation down her spine.

Determination on Lord Gordan's visage would be hard to deny. It was any wonder he was a renowned rakehell for who could refuse sin when offered to you in a rich, titled, handsome marquess package that was his lordship?

One could not.

The following morning Sarah broke her fast in her room, preferring not to dine with all the other guests. No doubt, Hugh and Molly would ask her about her absence later, but she could not sit across the table and see him.

Giles...

She may never be able to meet his gaze again after allowing him liberties last evening that she should not. Sarah sat before her dressing table, her maid pinning up the last of her curls, and she stared at her features, her lips that had been kissed most ardently, even now they tingled in remembrance. The shadows beneath her eyes told her the effect Lord Gordan had on her. Her sleep had been restless, her body not able to settle and rest.

She pursed her lips. Lord Gordan had done that to her, and he probably damn well knew he would. All she could hope was that he, too, had a sleepless night and resembled hell also.

He did not.

Sarah ran into his lordship, striding in from the back of the house a little after leaving her room. His boots were wet with melting snow, some of which was still sticking to his shoes. His tan breeches hugged his athletic thighs, and her mouth dried at the sight. Her eyes devoured his every article of clothing, the perfectly tied Napoleon cravat, and his top hat held loosely in one hand. His tan coat and white waistcoat giving him the air of a country gentleman, innocent and able. He may be able, but innocent was the opposite of what Giles was.

He glanced up, skidding to a stop. He met her inspection, and something inside her crumbled just as it had when she was fifteen.

Sarah had a name for the emotion that coursed through her blood back then. It had been love, innocent and adoring, but now it was laced with so many more conflicting sentiments—desire one of them. Anger, most definitely, but passion above all.

This month-long house party just became a whole lot longer.

CHAPTER 4

Giles skidded to a stop, seeing Sarah watching him. He'd missed her at breakfast, having observed that she was not at the table, he'd eaten quickly and gone for a ride before the mid-morning breeze picked up and made it too bitter to go outside.

He'd needed a good, brisk ride this morning, if only to wake himself up. After his kiss with Sarah, his sleep had been deprived most severely.

He'd tossed and turned and thought about taking himself in hand to alleviate the need that coursed through his blood.

The idea of Sarah in his bed would not abate, and it was a problem he needed to face.

He was a friend to her brother, but also one of town's most notorious rakes. All thanks to Lady Rackliffe, but the idea of taking Edith or anyone else to his bed left a sour taste in his mouth.

The only woman he wanted beneath him, on top of him, before him and every way else he could think of was Sarah.

It was a damnable, vexing notion since he'd only kissed her last night to prove that she did, in fact, care what he did, a mistake he realized the moment their lips touched. He'd most certainly proved a point, however, one that he was a fool. He would long for her until he kissed her again if she would allow him to.

"Lord Gordan, good morning. I hope you had a pleasant ride."

Her benign chatter did not mislead him, and he crossed his arms, taking in her pretty, plum gown with a gold thread about the seams. His eyes dipped to her abundant cleavage, and he wrenched his gaze upward before she caught him ogling. "I did, thank you for asking, Lady Sarah. Pray, tell me, how did you sleep last night? I hope it was to your satisfaction?"

Two could play this game of mundane conversation, and he would win. He rarely lost with anything—innocuous chatter with women he wanted in his bed no different.

She pursed her lips, and he knew she saw through his question. "I slept very well, thank you."

He raised his brow. "Actually, I lie. I managed very little rest at all. Do you have any idea as to why that could be so?"

Her inspection of him was thorough, her gaze skimming from his neck to his shoulders, taking in his crossed arms, to his abdomen and beyond.

What on earth was she looking at?

He glanced at himself, and seeing nothing untoward, frowned. "Is there something the matter with my clothing, my lady?"

She seemed to shake herself from her musings. "Not at all, my lord."

"So you're just admiring the view then?" he teased, catching her eye that dipped once again to his cravat. Her cheeks bloomed a pretty pink, and she moved past him, heading toward the back of the house.

He followed, the reasons as to why foreign to him. All he did know was that he didn't want their conversation to end and nor did he like that she could dismiss him so easily after their kiss the night before.

To Giles, that kiss had meant everything, changed everything in his life, and what he wanted.

Sarah, to be exact.

She used to care for him a lot. There had been a time when they would partake in many outings and adventures at this very estate.

Sarah entered a music room, a grand piano and harp occupying a corner each. Chairs sat about the instruments. Giles paused at the room's threshold, having not been in here for many years, not since Sarah's father had played for them all one Christmas a lifetime ago.

Sarah moved between the two instruments and sat on a padded window seat that overlooked the now-frozen-over lake, the snow falling heavily outdoors.

"You'll catch your chill sitting there."

She glanced at him as if she'd forgotten his presence. He ground his teeth. How could she be immune to him? Women never were, and once she had not been either. She had thrown herself at him, had, from what he could presume, wished for marriage.

Of course, he did not expect her to be pining for him all these years later, but they could surely be friends. From that footing, love could grow, he was sure of it.

Giles strode over, coming to a stop before her. He

waited for her to look up, needed to see her clear, green eyes and make her understand that he was in earnest. That she was different from his past lovers. That with Sarah, he wanted a future as well as a past.

"I apologize for kissing you last evening without your consent. I'm sorry that I did not kiss you back when we kissed all those years ago, but surely, with all that our lives have been intertwined, we can be friends. I want to be in your life, Sarah. Not as a lover, or childhood friend, but as a man you can come to, one who'll support your opinions and ideas just as I used to. When you told me of them, that is." He took her hand, squeezing it a little. "Please tell me we can be so again. I have missed you."

Sarah regarded Giles. She pushed down the hope that bloomed in her soul at his words. He wished to be friends. Then where had he been all these years? She'd certainly been right here at St. Albans Abbey. He was the one who had not visited, not reached out to see if she was well.

Which she had not been.

Not with a brother like Henry whom she had been left with after Hugh fled England. Her brother had been dismissive, short-tempered, and scandalous.

Whenever he'd held house parties, she had to retreat to the dowager house if only to protect herself from his wayward, bastard friends. Not that she'd always been safe even there.

She shuddered at the memory of Lord Fairchild and his pursuit of her, his inappropriate words, and eventually his insistence that she allow him to kiss her. Sarah had fled to Bath without a backward glance and had not seen Henry until the day she laid him to rest. A carriage accident brought on by more reckless behavior.

"A little late now, do you not think, to take an interest in my life. Where have you been the last ten years, my lord?" Sarah reached over to a nearby chair and picked up a shawl left there for her use. "When Henry had thrown house parties, I always hoped that you would attend so that we may move on from my inappropriate kiss, but you never did. You never called in on your way home to Willowood Hall. Nor did you write. I think you're a hypocrite, so why would I want to be your friend?"

Giles flinched at her words, but what did he expect? Turning up at a Christmas house party held by her brother did not mean all was forgiven. Not by her at least. She could not excuse his actions at leaving her alone.

"You gave me the cut direct the remainder of the 1819 Season," he accused.

"You scolded me at the beginning of that Season after I kissed you. Why would I follow you about like a little lost puppy looking for attention? I may have been young and naive, Lord Gordan, but I'm not a fool. I know when I'm not wanted."

"I did want you. You were all that I did want," he admitted.

Sarah shook her head, not believing his words, not wanting to see the yearning on Giles's face. Denying him what her own torturous body craved was almost impossible with him looking at her so. To believe the truth to his words would only cause heartache for her in the future. There was nothing between them, had not been for an eon. It was time they stopped this silly game they were playing. The Christmas festivities had addled both their minds and was teasing them with impossible dreams.

Giles sat beside her, and she shuffled over a little. "No you did not. You would have kissed me back, married me instead of offering to Lady Rackliffe. You may have missed our friendship, but you were merely missing a woman you saw more like your sister than anything of a deeper, emotional level."

"I never saw you as a sister, and I do want you. It may have taken me ten years to say the words, but I'm saying them now."

"You need to halt your silly declaration." Sarah went to stand, and he pulled her back down on the window seat beside him.

"It's not trivial, it's true. Our kiss last evening was proof of how much I want you, surely you felt what can be between us. Give me a chance."

Sarah swallowed, her heart and mind a firestorm of debate. Of course, she felt what they could have, from the tips of her ears to the ends of her toes she'd felt the fire that had coursed through her blood at his touch. If she gave him a chance to court her, what did that mean? Would it lead anywhere? She had thought him truthful and honorable during her first Season, and how wrong she had been then. There was just as much chance now that he was fooling her yet again, playing her like the instruments that sat about them.

Even so, the flash of determination in his eyes gave her pause. Perhaps Giles was sincere, and this Christmas, she may get what her heart truly longed for.

Was she brave enough to risk her heart a second time? "Very well," she said, pulling her hand free from his. "I will give you a chance to prove you are sincere, Lord Gordan, but mark my words, this is your final time. I will not be gifting another."

His wicked smile somersaulted butterflies in her stomach, and she had a moment of panic at what she'd unleashed. "I will not need any more chances, Sarah. I will not make the same mistake twice."

CHAPTER 5

The following day Sarah's attention was fixated on Giles as he spoke with her sister-in-law, Molly before the hearth in the front parlor. The snow had continued to fall, forcing Molly, as the hostess, to come up with varied and fun ways to pass the time inside.

They played card games, billiards, charades, and danced. Even so, how Giles would woo her to his favor was something Sarah was looking forward to.

No matter what she had said to his face, she had missed her old friend, and the fun they used to have. She looked forward to seeing this other side that only the privileged few managed to observe—his seductive, courting side.

Whatever would he do to convince her his heart was hers to steer?

"You're grinning like a fool. What are you up to, Sarah?"

She started at the sound of her brother's voice, jumping back a little to stop spilling her mulled wine on her light-green gown. "Nothing at all. Why would I be up to anything?"

"Because you are, and I know it."

Sarah chuckled, not wanting anyone, least of all her brother, to know that she was getting reacquainted with Giles. The last thing she needed was to become the latest tidbit of gossip for London's *ton*. They had used their family enough for that.

"It is Christmas, Hugh. Everyone is more jovial at this time of year," she said, leaning up and kissing his cheek. How different it was to last year's Christmas where she had spent it alone here at the Abbey. Henry having decided to stay in town instead of returning home. He should have come home, had he done so he may not have died only a few weeks into the new year.

Her Christmas luncheon had been a sad affair, with only herself at the table, the memory of chewing her food while tears streamed down her face was not one recollection she wished to keep.

"Sarah?" Hugh said, taking her hand and pulling her close. "What happened to your smile?"

She rallied, squeezing his hand, and smiling for good effect. Her isolation was not Hugh's fault, and he did not need the guilt plaguing him over her sad life up to the point of his return.

He was here now, she was happy, and as much as she did not wish to be bombarded with Londoners for the Christmas season, she was glad the house was at least full, with lots of laughter and fun. No worries of the guests behaving inappropriately or trying to persuade her to a rendezvous.

Of course, except for Giles, but a stolen kiss or two between two people who were courting wasn't so very bad.

"All is well, brother. I'm just so very happy you're home. I have missed you at this time of year."

He leaned over and kissed her cheek. "I missed you too. Promise me we shall never spend another Christmas apart."

"I can promise you that," she said, smiling. Her brother was called to another group of guests, and Sarah let him go. This afternoon Molly had organized a snowman competition, if the snow stopped falling that was. Sarah was looking forward to winning and going outside. They had spent too many days indoors as it was.

A tinkling sounded, and Sarah turned to see Molly calling everyone's attention with a small, golden bell.

"The snow has eased, and so I think that if we're to have this snowman building competition, we should do so now. So please, everyone, go and change into your warmest coats and boots and meet me and His Grace on the terrace where we shall notify you of your teammate."

Sarah did as she was bade, and within the hour, everyone assembled before the terrace doors. Over her green morning gown she had thrown on a fur jacket and scarf, and kid-leather gloves. Sturdy leather boots and a hat finished off her outfit.

"There will be a prize, of course," Molly continued. "Ten pounds and the honor of opening the Christmas ball with a waltz with a partner of your choice. As to whom you will be building your snowman with, the following guests, please team up."

Sarah listened as Molly named the guests. Those who were married were kept together while those unattached were paired.

"Lady Sarah Farley and Lord Gordan, please pair up."

Sarah shivered at the thought of being near him again and turned to seek him out. A hand slid across her back and down her arm. His fingers clasped hers, placing her hand on his arm.

She shot him a glance, having not known he was so near.

"Your muff is most complimentary."

Heat suffused her cheeks, and she stared at him, nonplussed. "From the tone of your voice, I cannot help but think you're saying something inappropriate, my lord."

His wicked grin undid her stoic sensibilities and proved her point. "That's because I am being immodest."

Sarah shook her head, turned back to her sister-in-law, and listened to the other guests still being paired. At the announcement that Lady Rackliffe was matched with the eligible earl, Lord Ambrose, Sarah took in her reaction. The earl had entered society the same year as them. He was a handsome gentleman and kind, and his pleasure at being paired with Lady Rackliffe was obvious.

Her displeasure, too, was most evident.

"We only have a limited time, a half hour at most before we need to return indoors, so I wish you well and good luck on your snowmen."

Two footmen opened the terrace doors and let the guests file outside. Sarah waited for the rush to subside before stepping outdoors. Chilly air made her catch her breath, and she pulled her scarf higher about her neck to stop the chill. Giles was beside her, his long greatcoat and highly polished riding boots made him appear taller than normal, wider across the shoulders and altogether too handsome in his beaver hat and leather gloves.

Sarah rallied her thoughts away from his handsome self and concentrated on the task at hand. "We must win this," she said, piling snow together into a ball. "I will not lose this competition, especially at my own home."

"And I shall not let you lose, Lady Sarah."

They worked together, piling snow up and up, rounding off the snowman's belly before moving on to his head. Some of the guests had already finished, their smaller men in no way grand enough to win, while others seemed too keen to rush and not compact the snow well enough, leaving it to crumble when the head was positioned.

Not theirs, however. Their snowman was strong, almost half Sarah's height and better than anyone else's she was sure.

"You will have to make yours bigger, Lady Sarah, if you wish to beat me," Lady Rackliffe shouted, laughing at her own words.

Sarah growled at the sight of her ladyship's tall snowman, compact and just as good as theirs. "Go and fetch some sticks for his arms and nose. I'll collect the stones for his eyes and mouth."

Giles nodded, running off to do her bidding. For a moment, she lost herself watching him trudge through the snow. Was the man destined to look perfect in any life situation he found himself? He was taller than most men she knew, and always, in her opinion, the most handsome. The thought that he wanted her above anyone else left her breathless, her heart pounding like it had the night she kissed him. With his golden locks, and devilish, wicked mouth he'd intoxicated her from the moment she'd first set eyes on him at the susceptible age of fourteen.

A snowball flew past, and the resulting scream when the snowball found its mark reminded her of her task. She ran over to a nearby garden, searched as best she could under the dormant rose bushes for small rocks. Finding only a few small pebbles, she ran back to the snowman, placing them on his mouth and face. Molly called out that they only had ten minutes left, and Sarah took stock of the other entrants they were up against.

Lord Ambrose took off his scarf and wrapped it about the snowman, and Sarah frowned. They would have to do something similar if they wanted to win. Giles returned with his sticks, thin ones that suited the arms and nose well.

Sarah stepped up next to Giles and slid the scarf from his neck. A lazy, tempting smile tweaked his lips as he stood there, allowing her to de-clothe him. Her skin prickled in awareness before she rose on her toes and, holding his shoulders for support, slipped his hat off as well.

"You're awfully close, my lady. Are you trying to tempt me out here in the freezing air? Because it's warming my blood to no end."

Unable not to, she chuckled, shaking her head at his words. It wasn't any wonder women fell at this rogue's feet. He was amusing and wicked and reminded her of the fun-loving young man who had enchanted her all those years ago.

"If you kissed me out here before everyone, you would have to marry me."

He wiggled his brows, and she smiled. "Is that so very bad? I could think of worse fates."

Lady Rackliffe caught her attention by taking the jacket off Lord Ambrose as well, telling him without question that it must be so for them to win.

Giles heard her ladyship's words and cringed. "Please tell me I'm not going to have to part with my coat as well, my lady. I do believe winning at that cost is too high."

He turned back, and she sighed, agreeing with his lordship even though she would have taken his jacket should he have offered.

"Very well, I will not disrobe you entirely."

Giles watched her for a moment, his eyes full of mirth. He was so very good-looking. How fortunate he was to be blessed with such angelic features that left a woman's heart to flutter.

Molly called time, and her sister-in-law and brother walked about the group of snowmen before declaring Lady Rackliffe the winner.

Her ladyship jumped in glee, clapping her hands and laughing at the announcement before coming over to Sarah and Giles. Sarah took in the sway of her ladyship's hips, her overly bright smile, and knew it for what it was. She was determined to make Lord Gordan hers once more. The heavy-lidded gaze that promised whatever Giles wanted was clear for all to see.

"Lord Gordan, I must ask if you would be willing to open the Christmas ball with me. It has been so very long since we waltzed together. Too long," she whispered for only Giles to hear. Sarah heard her words too, the idea of anyone in Giles's arms but herself making her temper soar.

Giles looked about those who strolled past, heading back indoors before meeting Sarah's eyes. He stuttered his answer, and Sarah took pity on him. "I'm sure Lord Gordan would be honored, my lady. Shall we return inside? It is starting to get quite brisk outdoors."

Sarah turned without seeing if they followed, but she could hear the crunch of their shoes in the snow that told her they did. Sarah ground her teeth, having wanted to dance the waltz with Giles herself.

She continued through the drawing room, determined to find their butler, who would be acting as the major-domo for the ball. This year, the St. Albans Christmas ball would have two waltzes, not one.

CHAPTER 6

Giles escaped the house party later that afternoon. He stepped out the servant's back door, pulling his greatcoat closed, the brisk, afternoon air as cold as an arctic blast. He started toward the stables with quickened steps, noting the stable doors were closed. He let himself inside via a smaller side door, grateful to be out of the inclement weather.

The air inside the stables was a lot warmer, the building so well made that not a cold draft or freezing drop of rain penetrated the space.

A cooing and light, feminine chatter caught his attention, and frowning, he moved forward along the stalls, looking into each one to see who was there. Warmth speared through his blood at the sight of Sarah brushing her mount, her hands running along the flank of the sixteen-hand chestnut after each stroke of her brush.

The sight of her hands stroking the animal's flesh should not tempt him, but it did. From the moment she'd kissed him in London all those years ago, he'd thought of little else. Every woman he'd ever bedded, flirted with at entertainments, sated his lust with, all bore a striking resemblance to Sarah, and he knew the reason why.

He'd wanted her above everyone else from the moment their lips had touched.

His father, a proud and strict gentleman, would not allow his courtship of her due to her being Lord Hugh Farley's sibling. He'd been told in terms that brooked little argument that Lady Sarah was not suitable for the Gordan family, no matter her rank, and for him to look elsewhere unless he wanted to live life penniless.

He should have called his father's bluff, tested him on his words, and offered to Sarah anyway. He may have become poor as a result, but there was one thing his father could not take from him, and that was the title he would eventually inherit. Sarah herself was not without funds. They would have survived. A foolish mistake and one he would regret always.

Giles leaned over the stable door, content to watch her coo to her horse and enjoy her solitary time away. He wished he'd stood up to his father and told him that the rumors against Hugh were unfounded and possibly untrue, which they were proven to be in the end. That Lady Sarah was innocent of any slight.

That his sire had persuaded him to offer to Edith, now Lady Rackliffe, and he had, was an action that even he would find hard to excuse.

When Sarah had kissed him, but a day after his betrothal, he'd been so livid, not at Sarah, but himself for choosing the wrong woman. He'd lashed out, punished Sarah with words that had been untrue. Hurt the one woman he had wanted simply because he could not change the error of his ways.

He did not deserve her now, not after making her wait

all this time, but he could not leave her be. A fire burned in his soul, and it was only Sarah who could extinguish it.

He wanted her.

Giles cleared his throat. "We missed you after luncheon. I did not know that you were hiding out here in the stables, or I would have joined you sooner."

Sarah walked about the back of her horse, pushing the mare across a little so she could brush the opposite side. "You should know that I often escape out here. The staff has been allowed the day to join their families for the festive season, and so I'm checking on the horses instead. They'll be back later this evening, but I needed to brush Opie in any case."

Giles watched her work the brush over the horse's back, the mare calm, her head lowered and her eyes barely open. "You're putting your horse to sleep."

Sarah chuckled, and the sound did odd things to him. He wanted to hear her laugh, her jovial voice, for the rest of his life. If he could persuade her to love him as he hoped she once had, their lives could be perfect.

"She relishes a good brush." Sarah slipped under the horse's neck, coming to stand before him. "What are you doing out here, my lord? I thought you would be too busy with Lady Rackliffe following you about every minute of every day to escape to the stables."

Was that jealousy he heard in her tone? He narrowed his eyes, shrugging. "Lady Rackliffe is happily situated indoors. I wanted to find you."

Sarah reached over the wooden door, sliding the lock across to let herself out. "Her ladyship will be most unhappy to have lost the company of her preferred."

"I'm not her preferred."

She laughed again. This time, he did not miss her

mocking tone. "Oh, yes, you are. She's quite determined to secure you. However will you evade her charms? From what I remember, you were quite taken with them once before."

Giles helped her shut the stable door before bolting it closed. "That was a long time ago. She's not whom I want."

A light blush stole across her cheeks before she stepped around him, evading his eyes and his company. Giles followed her to the back of the stables to where a large pile of hay was stacked and strewn over the floor.

She turned, lifting her chin and once again was a duke's daughter, proud and confident. "What are you doing out in the stables, my lord? Are you going to help me give the horses some feed, or did you come out to go for a ride? I do not want to hold you up in any way."

He had intended going for a ride, but the idea was no longer so tempting. Not with Sarah keeping him company. "I will help, most gladly." Giles helped her load biscuits of hay for each horse, check their water and stalls for any steaming piles. After filling the last of the horse's water, he turned to find Sarah sitting on the hay, watching him, her eyes bright with amusement.

"You're laughing at me, why is that?" he asked, washing his hands in a small bowl, before striding over to her.

She grinned. "No reason. I just like seeing you like this. It reminds me of how we used to be when doing things together. Do you remember?"

"I do." He flopped down next to her, leaning back to look up at the wooden rafters above them, the hay acting as a barrier against the cold. Giles had to admit that right at this moment, his blood was heated. No doubt due to the fact he was with Sarah and quite alone at that. "There was nothing better than to explore the wilderness about the estate. I keep meaning to visit the fort out in the woods."

"It's still there." She leaned back next to him, her attention also on the roof.

Giles took the opportunity to watch her, taking in the pretty sweep of her nose, full lips, and faultless skin. He'd dreamed about her so often, but having her near, hearing her voice was so much better than any fantasy.

"I believe the sword you and Hugh carved is also. In the summer, I still use the fort. It's a wonderful place to read and not be disturbed."

"Your father was a clever man. I never doubted that it was not still standing."

She smiled at him, and his stomach clenched. She was so very close. He wanted to lean across the small space that separated them and kiss her. To do so would be dangerous, considering their current status, but even so, the pull to have her in his arms was overwhelming.

He clenched his fists into the straw at his sides, forcing himself to court her slowly and not keep molesting her with every chance offered.

"He was, wasn't he?" She turned, studying him a moment. "How long are we going to lie here, my lord?"

Giles frowned, meeting her gaze. "Stay here? Did you wish to return to the house? We can, if that is your wish."

"No," she said, chuckling. "I meant to say, how long are we going to lie here before you kiss me, Giles? That is what I'd like to know."

CHAPTER 7

Sarah was well aware she was playing with fire. Lord Gordan was a reputed rake. A man made for pleasure and fun. Not a gentleman easily brought to heel.

Not that she wished to control him, but she could not bear to hear of any liaisons he had should they continue along this path of courtship. His absence from her life had been severing. To be married and know that one's husband was unfaithful would be unbearable.

Even so, lying beside him in the hay, watching as his eyes darkened with wicked intent, she couldn't help but throw herself into the wild. For so many years, she'd not lived as she ought to have, no more would she wither away, secluded in Kent or Bath.

With an elder brother who hosted scandalous parties and cared little for restraint and her other sibling abroad under a shadow of scandal, she had hidden away, not wanting to be any further embarrassment or fodder for town gossip.

Sarah had managed and accepted her lot in life as well

as anyone could in her position. But having Giles's dark-blue eyes all but devour her person as he closed the space between them, she knew to her very core that she was in trouble.

That allowing him such liberties would forever change her and her steadfast denial of her feelings for him that she had long bottled away, corked, and shelved.

His lips brushed hers, warm and soft, and a frisson of need coursed through her blood. He lifted his hand, pushing a lock of her hair behind her ear. "You're so beautiful. You may not believe me, but I've wanted you for so long. I attended each Season in town only to be disappointed when I heard you were not attending."

Sarah clasped his nape, sliding her hand up into his soft, golden locks. She steeled herself not to be carried away by his words. Their friendship had been distant for so long. It would take time for her to adjust to his enlightenment of what they could have. To trust him as she once had.

"Why did you never attend one of Henry's house parties then, or call at the Abbey? You knew I was here. You knew I was alone."

Pain crossed his features as she waited for his answer. "I wanted to come and see you. So much, Sarah, but my father kept me busy elsewhere and always demanded I attend the Season and stay in town."

"Had you been able to see me, what would you have said?" *Or done?* The question hovered on her lips and between them. She wanted to know would he have acted sooner. Defied his father for her had he seen her face-to-face. It was a lot harder to deny one's feelings when standing before the person one cared for.

"I should have done what I've wanted to for so long."

He kissed her again, urging her to lie on the straw. She adjusted her position as little prickly stalks jabbed through the jacket over her gown. The feel of his tongue begging entry made her gasp, and he delved into her mouth. Warmth settled between her thighs, and she squeezed her legs a little, trying to stem her need. How was it that this man, an enemy only a week before, could make her so willing in his arms?

The kiss turned heated, his demands raw and hard, and unlike anything she'd ever experienced before. Her senses reeled, her breath hitched. She relished Giles like this. A little wild and without restraint. Sarah clasped the lapels of his jacket, holding him against her. His hand slid down her waist, his clever fingers sliding across to tease the undersides of her breasts, but no farther. Frustration made her whimper, and she pushed against him, wanting his hand to move, to kneed her aching flesh.

With each breath she took, her gown scraped against her nipples, spiking pleasure and want. She craved the feel of his hands upon her person. It didn't matter as to where so long as he gave her what she wanted.

His manhood settled against her core, and she whimpered, a spike of pleasure making her wet. Even with the abundance of skirts and multiple petticoats and two layers of stockings, Sarah could feel the substantial size of him. His hardness tempted her to squirm and rub up against him like a house cat looking for a good scratch.

She gasped, breaking the kiss, needing to calm her racing heart. Giles did not stop his assault. Oh no, he kissed his way down her neck, his tongue and teeth teasing her earlobe. The heavenly sensation wrought her senses to flee, and she lay back, welcoming him to do more, to take her if he wished, just so long as the delicious sensations coursing across her body right at that moment never ended.

"You're so beautiful, Sarah." Giles breathed in the sweet-smelling scent of roses her skin always held. He would forever love the pretty, petaled flower for the reminder of her.

His body roared with need, his cock hard and primed. Sarah's legs wrapped tightly about his waist as he rocked into her, sliding his cock against her cunny. Oh god, it felt good. Too good to stop even though they could be walked in on at any moment.

He was a rutting bastard to tease her, in a stable no less, but he could not halt. Did not want to pause the delicious heat that coursed down his spine and threaded into his groin. His balls tightened, release all but imminent.

Her fingers scored down his back through his great-coat. Her little mewls of need told him he could make her come this way. The light flush on her cheeks and eyes heavy-lidded with passion were all he needed to know she was at the point of no return.

Giles slowed his undulation against her, needing to drag out their interlude. She moaned, closing her eyes, and the sight of her enjoyment almost undid his control.

"You approve, my darling?" he whispered against her ear, licking it for good measure and eliciting a gasp from her kissable lips.

"Yes," she sighed, pushing against him and meeting his every stroke.

He bit down on the inside of his mouth, stemming his release. He could not continue to tease for much longer, not unless he wanted to walk back into the house with a stain at the front of his pants.

"You make me want so much, Sarah."

"You make me need too," she said, her words a whispered sigh of delight.

Giles reached down, lifting her leg higher on his hip. The urge to hoist up her gown, rip open his falls and fuck her, here in the stable, overwhelmed his senses. His control strained to a snapping point.

The sound of men's voices sounded outside the stable walls. The thought of being caught in such a situation doused his desire like sand on hot coals, and Giles wrenched up off Sarah, pulling her to stand as he did so.

Confusion clouded her sweet face, and he quickly checked her gown, removing the pieces of hay that he could see were stuck in her hair. She didn't help, merely stared at him, her eyes wide and heavy-lidded with unsated desire. He grinned, knowing he'd discombobulated her to the point of silence.

Giles dragged them before one of the horse's stalls, putting space between them. He leaned over the door, making it seem as if they were discussing the horse stabled inside. The stable doors slid open and in walked three men, one of whom Giles recognized as the head stableman.

"Good afternoon, my lord, Lady Sarah," Bruce, the eldest and most superior of the three, said, tipping his hat.

"Good afternoon," Sarah said, stepping away from Giles and heading for the door. "I hope you enjoyed your afternoon with your families. Did they savor the hams we sent over?"

Bruce pulled his cap off his head, holding it before him, a wide, genuine smile playing about his mouth. "It was most extravagant, my lady. We thank you and His Grace for your kindness."

Giles watched as Sarah reached out, clasping the older man's arm in affection. "You are most welcome, and it was our pleasure."

She left them then, and Giles remembered that he had come out for a ride, but no longer wanted to. Watching Lady Sarah saunter out of sight, he could not think of anyone he'd prefer to ride at this very moment other than her.

He bid the workers a good afternoon and set out after her, determined to finish what they had started.

CHAPTER 8

Sarah did not make it very far into the house when she was dragged into the drawing room to have her likeness sketched by Lady Sebastian, who was renowned for her lifelike drawings of people using crayons.

Molly came to sit beside her, chattering of the house party and their plans over the coming days. Her closest friends were seated about them, watching as Sarah had her likeness drawn, they too busy with ideas for the new duchess.

Sarah absently listened as they gossiped and laughed about the past Season and the new one to come. What milestones their children had achieved and the Christmas Ball here at the Abbey, which was coming up.

None of the conversation points drew Sarah in. Nothing would, she was sure. After what she had experienced in the stables with Giles, she doubted she would ever be so again.

Who knew that a man could create a riot of sensations throughout her body, make her want to throw away her well-behaved self and see what else Giles could make her feel?

He was utterly a master at seduction, and she'd been only too ready for a tryst in the hay like some housemaid too free with her favors.

Sarah glanced up and met the eyes of the Duchess of Carlisle. She schooled her features, not liking the knowing tilt of the duchess's lips. Heat suffused her face. Why was Her Grace looking at her so? Did she know something about her venture with Giles only a short time ago?

Impossible, and yet, something told Sarah Her Grace was more perceptive than the others and saw something different in her.

"Oh my, Lady Sarah, the sketch is positively breathtaking. You look most beautiful and natural in this image," Marchioness Ryley said, standing behind Lady Sebastian as she continued to draw.

Molly walked about the easel and took in the image, her attention snapping to Sarah, a contemplative look in her eye. Oh no, not her sister-in-law too!

"Very interesting indeed. I think you shall like the likeness, Sarah," Molly said, smiling at her.

Lady Sebastian set down the crayon she was using and surveyed her drawing with pride. "I think it captures Lady Sarah honestly." Her ladyship picked up the parchment, handing it to Sarah. "Here you are, my dear, you may do with this drawing as you wish."

Sarah took the sketch and studied it, a croak of distress lodging in her throat at what she saw. Did she truly look to others as Lady Sebastian had expressed her?

Her cheeks were flush with color, her hair not as pristine as some of the other ladies present, and why would it be after a romp in the hay? Her lips were a deep shade of pink, and swollen. She bit her lip, her body remembering the passionate embrace and wanting more. Her eyes held a faraway expression as if she were still in Lord Gordan's arms.

Where she belonged...

Sarah lifted her hand to her cheek, feeling the heat from her blush on her fingers. Oh, dear Lord. Did Molly suspect? Duchess Carlisle certainly did, she feared.

"Thank you," she said, standing and starting for the door. "I'm most grateful and will cherish it always."

Sarah fled the room, not bothering with an explanation as to why. She smiled in welcome to the few gentlemen who milled about the foyer, some of them heading toward the drawing room. No doubt, they had been playing billiards or taking part in the gaming room that Hugh had set up for the duration of the house party.

Her room's safety beckoned, a place where she could hide the drawing from anyone else having to see. What would they think if they knew the truth? That Lady Sebastian had captured her every thought, her every desire, and crushing need that coursed through her blood still, after being with Giles in the stable.

She was almost to her room when a gentleman who came out of the servants' stairs stopped her dead in her tracks. Giles moved into the passage, unaware of her rushing to her room. He glanced up, pleasure filling his features and leaving her breathless once again.

"Sarah." He came up to her and, checking they were alone, lifted a sprig of mistletoe above her head. He leaned down and stole a kiss. "I missed you now."

He stood back, his gaze latching on to the drawing. "May I see it?" he asked.

Sarah swallowed the nerves that tumbled about her

belly at having this attractive, eligible lord, hers to do with as she pleased, before her again. "It's a silly sketch, nothing to mind." Sarah did not want him to see it, or anyone else. If Giles saw the expression on her face, reminiscing about her escapades with his lordship, he would know her secret.

That no matter what she said otherwise, no matter how much of a wall she built up around herself when it came to the man before her, he merely needed to clap his hands, and she came to attention.

Silly little fool that she was, she could not help herself. She wanted him. Had wanted Giles for years and wished that he'd been her knight in shining armor, the man who rode to St. Albans Abbey and saved her from her self-isolated fate.

He had not. No one had. Her brother Henry had made sure of that with his scandalous escapades in town after Hugh left.

He tipped his head to the side. "Let me see it, Sarah. I will not show anyone." He reached for the drawing, and she jerked it away.

"Did you draw it yourself?" he asked after a moment.

"No." She shook her head, her cheeks flaming. "I need to freshen up."

He grinned, knowing full well why she needed to bathe and dress for dinner. "Please let me see?"

He spoke in a soothing, cajoling voice, and she sighed, holding the sketch out to him. Not able to deny him anything, it would seem, for very long. "Very well, but do not say a word about it. I need no commentary on the likeness."

. . .

Giles took the parchment, holding up the sketch to take in the image. His mouth dried at the sight of Sarah, the distant light in her eyes, the knowing, wicked grin on her swollen lips.

He cleared his throat. "When was this drawn?"

Sarah crossed her arms over her chest. "Lady Sebastian was doing them in the drawing room just now."

The image of Sarah made his gut clench. Never had he thought an artist could capture a moment in someone's life so well, but Lady Sebastian certainly had. Sarah looked every bit a woman who had been thoroughly ravished. A woman who also enjoyed every lascivious, sinful moment of it.

He licked his lips, remembering their tryst in the stable. "May I keep it?" He would treasure it until the time came that he could have another one done of Sarah when she was his wife, and he was beside her.

"You cannot." She snatched it out of his hand, placing it behind her back. "What if someone sees you with it? They will ask questions."

He shrugged, nonplussed. "So what if they do?"

Sarah checked the passage for guests before rounding on him. "People will suspect if you have the drawing that there is something between us."

"There is something between us," he said, leaning down and whispering against her lips. He met her startled eyes, winking. "I want there to be something between us, Sarah. After what happened in the stables, I thought you would understand that more than any other."

"Ho, Gordan, I have been looking for you."

Sarah gasped, stepping back as if she were threatened by hot coals, her back coming up hard against the door.

Giles turned, smiling at Hugh, who strode toward them. "Albans, I too was just coming to find you," he lied, having had no intention. Truth be told, he was about to prove that he wanted Sarah in his life in every possible way that he could.

In his room. Alone, if she were willing.

"Come, man, we're about to start a game of billiards, and I need you to make up the numbers. All the other fellows are too busy cozying up to the ladies in the drawing room."

Giles nodded. "Of course," he said, bowing quickly to Sarah, before starting down the hall.

Hugh lingered, looking at the drawing that Sarah clutched behind her back. "I see you had your likeness sketched, Sarah. May I see it?" Hugh held out his hand, and Giles watched as Sarah stared at his appendage as if it were some crazed body part.

"No, I'm sorry. I will see you at dinner," she said, rushing into her room and shutting the door with a decided slam.

Hugh turned to stare at Giles, a frown between his brow. "Whatever is wrong with her, do you suppose?" Hugh approached Giles as he moved toward the stairs, knowing it was better to answer this question than Sarah, who seemed to be struggling with whatever was happening between them.

Affection. Enjoyment. Pleasure...

"I believe she is tired. I ran into her earlier at the stables. Maybe she needs a rest before dinner this evening."

"Yes, perhaps you're right." Hugh sighed. "Sisters, I will have to get used to having one again after all this time. Even so, I shall check in on her tonight to ensure she is well."

Giles didn't reply, not wanting to give Hugh any reason to suspect him of anything. Not yet, at least. He needed to win over Sarah before he won over his friend. "Tell me, who are we playing against?"

"Ah, Whitstone, and Duncannon. Both of whom believe we require a good trouncing."

Giles scoffed. "We shall see about that." He never liked to lose, not in a game of billiards or life. By the end of the Christmas house party, he too would win Sarah's heart.

Just as he had it ten years before.

CHAPTER 9

The following evening Sarah stood before the roaring hearth in the ballroom where some spontaneous dancing had been organized. The ladies took turns in playing the pianoforte for those who wished to dance while others had a turn about the room.

The room smelled of pine, one of the three Christmas trees at St. Albans Abbey stood in the corner of the room without decoration, the tradition of decorating the tree to happen Christmas eve.

A portion of the yule log burned in the grate. Sarah took in the many merry guests, conceding that it wasn't so bad to have all the guests stay at the estate. Over the few days that they had been here, they had been both kind and welcoming, not bringing up her time away or the reasons that occurred.

Hugh and Molly seemed to be enjoying themselves as well, and she couldn't help but wonder if they would return to Rome as much as they had stated they would. Certainly, they seemed very well placed here in Kent, with their new baby and marriage.

Sarah sipped her milk punch, her attention snapping to the door when Giles entered, Lady Rackliffe beside him, looking as pleased as she always did when around his lordship.

A prickle of annoyance threaded through her at the sight of them together. They made a handsome pair, both light-haired, attractive, and titled, should a marriage happen between them, they would be a highly placed couple in society.

So would you, should you marry Lord Gordan.

Sarah did not move, merely watched as Lady Rackliffe leaned up to whisper something in Giles's ear. He nodded before striding away.

Her hold on her crystal flute tightened before she took a calming breath, reminding herself that Giles had asked her to trust him, let him court her, not Lady Rackliffe. He would not play her the fool.

Her brother strode over to her, and she schooled her features, not wanting him to know anything about her muddled thoughts on Giles. "Sarah, my dear, I'm glad to catch you on your own. I wanted to talk to you about yesterday. You seemed a little distressed when I came upon you with Lord Gordan."

Sarah shook her head, wrapping her arm around Hugh's. "Nothing at all is wrong. I was merely tired after attending my horse in the stables. How did your billiards game go? I hope you won, as you wished to."

He smiled down at her, his eyes bright with happiness. "Of course. Whitstone was all talk when it came to his ability." Hugh chuckled. "Are you enjoying yourself? We have not left you alone too often, I hope. I do want our first Christmas together again to be a pleasant one."

"Not at all. Surprisingly, despite my earlier concerns, I

have enjoyed myself immensely. Everyone has been kind and not bold enough to bring up Henry and what he did. Have you found the same?"

He nodded, his face clouding a moment at the reminder of Henry and what he had done to Miss Cox and Hugh, especially. "I have. Molly seems to be the most accomplished hostess too. How lucky we are," he said, smiling down at her, the love he had for his wife shining in his eyes.

"Molly is simply the best choice you have ever made. If I have not said before, Hugh, I am so very happy for you both."

"Thank you, Sarah. Your words mean a lot to me." Hugh gestured to the dancers. "I hope you're going to partake in a jig or waltz this evening. The most handsome sister in attendance should not be a wallflower."

"Perhaps I will." She grinned, hoping that Giles would move over to where she stood and ask her.

Hugh studied her a moment, a small frown between his brows. "You have been spending some time with Lord Gordan these past few days. Each time I look up, you're together partaking in conversation. Is there something that I should be aware of between you two?"

Heat rushed to her face, and she prayed he did not notice. "What? No, nothing is happening between his lordship and myself. We're friends, just as we once were."

"If I recall correctly, you had a falling out just after I left. Lord Gordan wrote to me and told me of his disappointment."

"What? He wrote to you and told you? What did he say?"

Hugh stared at her as if she had lost her mind, which,

if she found out that Giles had told Hugh of her kissing him, she may very well do.

"That you disagreed over a trivial matter, and you refused to speak to him. That is all he said."

Sarah sighed, swallowing her fear and mortification that what she had done to Giles others may know about. And not just anyone, but her brother. "That is all in the past now. I have moved on from that difference of opinion."

Hugh's lips lifted into a half smile. "I am glad for it, for I do believe Lord Gordan likes you, Sarah. More than you possibly know."

Oh no, she knew how much Giles liked her, and she had enjoyed every second of him showing her so yesterday in the stables. Even now, her body yearned for his touch, his kiss, his breathy gasps against her ear when he'd undulated against her flesh.

"We're friends. Of course, he admires me." She sipped her punch to stop from having to say any more.

"I'm not blind, sister. I have seen the way he watches you, waits for you when you're not present. He thinks that I do not discern, but I do."

Sarah made the mistake of being caught in her brother's penetrating stare. She bit her lip, thinking it best not to say anything at all lest she blurt out her fear that she was falling in love with the marquess. If it were not love, it most certainly was already lust.

"He does not look at me so. You're too overcome with Christmas festivity to see clearly," she teased.

He chuckled, the sound mocking. "I'm not blind, no matter what you may think. I ask for one thing if there is anything between you. Do not cause a scandal by doing anything untoward. There are many eyes on our family, thanks to Henry. We must not allow the *ton* to have any further fodder to use against us."

Sarah nodded, shamed by her brother's words. Had anyone come across her and Giles yesterday in the stables, she would have been ruined. Her family once again the main talking point of gossip in town. She would have been dragged down the aisle to become Lord Gordan's wife before she could explain what she was about.

Not that being his wife was ever so bad. There had been a time that she'd wanted that above anything else, but he had chosen another. That that other person happened to be at this house party was merely an inconvenience. Even so, it did not change the fact that he was now courting her, not anyone else.

If she behaved, waited to see where her newfound friendship with Giles led, maybe they would be married before the next Season. "I will not do anything that could cause you or Molly harm. I promise," she said to her brother, just as a shadow fell before them both.

Sarah glanced up, her stomach fluttering, and she knew who was before them before observing him for herself.

"Lord Gordan," she said, dipping into a curtsy. "I hope you've come to our little impromptu dance ready to escort many a young woman onto the boards."

His eyes bored into her, the heat that she could see swirling in his blue orbs sent a frisson of desire to pool at her core. The man before her was determined to throw her life into a delightful turmoil.

"I am, Lady Sarah." He held out his hand. "Will you do me the honor?"

Sarah looked up at her brother, and the knowing look he bestowed upon her told her all she needed to know. Her brother had seen and approved. All that was left was for her to decide if she also did.

Sarah placed her hand atop of Giles's arm. He covered her hand immediately with his own, leading her onto the dance floor. "What is the next dance, do you know?"

The strains of a waltz started, and he grinned, a devilishly wicked light in his eyes. "I never leave anything to chance, my lady. Now, come here," he said, pulling her into his arms.

Sarah went willingly. At this time, should he ask her of anything, she was sure she would do it.

Even say yes to this handsome marquess.

CHAPTER 10

Giles made sure he danced with every woman present at the impromptu ball that the Duke of St. Albans had organized. The Christmas ball was still a week away, but with the need to keep those in attendance happy and occupied, a small dance did not hurt any of the plans.

The main Christmas ball would have the families of the nobility who lived close by in attendance, a much grander and more formal affair.

He had danced with Sarah twice already and knew he should not ask again. His interest would be noted and would only bring more eyes watching them.

He didn't need that annoyance. He wanted to spend as much time as he could with Sarah without everyone watching their every move. He needed to make her trust that he was in earnest. Explain to her, when the time was right, why he'd not thrown Lady Rackliffe aside when Sarah had kissed him.

That his betrothed had thrown him over had been a

welcome reprieve from a choice he had not wanted to make in the first place.

Nothing stood in his way of having Sarah as his wife now. As much as he loved and missed his parents, they were no longer living, and he could choose whomever he wished.

The night was coming to an end, and he bid those about him goodnight, having already done so with Sarah before she took a turn about the floor with her brother.

Giles left the ballroom, heading for the servant's stairs over that of the main staircase. It came out just beside his suite of rooms, and there was less of a chance of him being accosted by Lady Rackliffe, who appeared determined to take up as much of his time as she could.

He pushed through the servant's stairwell door into the passage near his room, the paneled door unsuspecting to anyone walking up the corridor. A feminine gasp sounded, and he closed the door quickly to see Sarah looking at him as if he'd accosted her.

"Apologies, Sarah. I did not think any of the family were headed to bed as yet."

She clasped her chest, her eyes wide with fright. "You startled me, that is all. I wasn't expecting anyone to barrel through. What are you doing using the servant's stairs again?"

He glanced down the hall to ensure they were alone. "Avoiding Lady Rackliffe. She's quite determined to catch me under a bough of mistletoe."

Sarah's delightful mouth twisted into a mulish line. Was she jealous? Did she not like the thought of someone else vying for his attention? He could well understand the sentiment. He, too, did not want to think of Sarah being with anyone else but him. It had only been by chance that he'd stood by all the years to take over the title that she had not married.

Had he been a man, stood up to his father and demanded he was marrying whomever he liked, they could have possibly been married for several years by now.

But he had not. He'd been a coward. Had allowed his father's prejudice and threats to keep him away from her. Thank bloody Christ that he did not have that issue any longer.

He was a bastard to think that way, to be now able to court Sarah meant that his father was gone. Even so, his sire had been wrong to demand such from him. He would not do it to his son when the time came.

"Lady Rackliffe does seem determined. Now that she is a widow, you do not wish to try your advantage at winning her heart a second time?"

"Hell no," he said, his tone more severe than he'd meant to project.

Sarah started at his words, staring at him. "She will be disappointed," she said after a time.

Giles stepped closer to her, placing but a hairsbreadth between them. "Let her be. She is not the woman I want, as you well know."

Sarah's eyes twinkled with a knowing light, and his body yearned to pull her against him. Kiss her soundly until they were both sated.

"Did you enjoy dancing this evening? You were quite the popular gentleman."

"I aim to please." Giles reached out, the urge to touch her sweet face overwhelming. Her skin was soft and warm, and he ran his thumb along her jaw, swiping it over her bottom lip. Her lips opened on a sigh, and his body hardened. "I want to please you."

Sarah shivered at his words. She wanted him to please her, too, in all ways. Thoughts of being with him as they were yesterday afternoon flittered through her mind, made her body yearn and ache.

His stormy, blue eyes darkened, enticing and wicked as ever. She had been so very angry at him for so long, how was it that a mere kiss, a sweet word, and roguish touch could make her let go of what had happened between them?

Because you were old friends, you loved him once.

All true of course, she had loved him, had been his friend, until he tried to marry a woman even Sarah could have told him would not make him happy. Sarah had long believed it was only she who could make him so, and now, after all these years apart, it would seem she was correct in that estimation.

What was she to do about it?

"Please me as you did yesterday in the stable? I do believe that was teasing, not pleasing, my lord." Her naughty words were unlike anything she'd ever spoken before. But she could not stop herself. Her body was not her own. Not anymore. She wanted the man before her to finish what he had started in the hay.

A growl emitted from him, and her breath hitched. "You're playing with fire, Sarah. Do not tempt me. I'm already at my limit when it comes to you."

She raised her brow, wanting to stir him more. See where their interlude could end. "Really? So if I were to step closer to you…" Sarah did as she suggested, her body close against his, her breasts grazing his chest. Her nipples pebbled, and moisture pooled at her core when his hardness settled into the dip of her stomach.

Sarah bit her lip, reaching up to drape her arms about his shoulders. "Your tolerance would snap?"

"Fuck, yes, it would." He picked her up, walked two steps, and pushed her up against the paneled wall. His mouth settled over hers, deep and commanding, taking her lips with a punishing edge.

Sarah clasped his shoulders, let go of her inhibitions, and drank from his desire. Let it spark hers to a flame. His hands slid down her back, clutching at her dress as if to rip it from her person.

Desire and need thrummed through his actions, his strong hands shaking against her body told her without words what she did to him. He hoisted one of her legs against his hip at the same time he ground against her, reminiscent of yesterday.

Oh yes...

They moaned, and with a nip to her lip, Giles pulled back, staring at her as if he were unsure, uncertain of what they were doing. Sarah knew exactly what they were about, and she wasn't going to let him end this interlude before he finished what they had started.

"I shouldn't be doing this, Sarah. Not until we're married."

The word marriage acted like a balm against any fears she may have held. Sarah kissed him quickly, a light brushing of lips. "Make love to me, Giles. I do not want to go to bed alone."

He leaned his forehead against hers, his eyes pools of uncertainty and need.

"We cannot," he gasped as she rubbed against him, using him to soothe the ache between her legs.

Sarah pushed him away with one hand before sauntering toward his bedroom door. "Yes, we can, and you will. I've never heard the Marquess of Graham being a man who did not satisfy. Do not start now. Not with me."

CHAPTER 11

Giles followed Sarah into his room, shutting and locking the door to ensure they were not disturbed. She was a goddess, her gold silk gown with gauze shimmering over the fabric gave her an air of decadence and privilege, of beauty that was both outside and in.

She sat on the edge of his bed, her wicked, come-hither look she threw him threatening to buckle his knees.

Giles strode over to her, wrenching his cravat and jacket off, dropping them to the floor without a second thought. Within a few moments, he stood before her with nothing but his breeches, his bare feet refusing to move from the soft Aubusson rug.

"I'll need help with my gown," she said, leaning over and giving him her back.

He drank in the sight of her straight spine, her swan-like neck, and sun-kissed hair pulled up into a decorative motif.

Thoughts of pushing her onto her hands, racking up her gown, and taking her from behind bombarded his mind. Giles pushed down his baser, harsher needs. Sarah was a maid, her first time with him could not be so, but one day. Soon, he promised himself. They would enjoy other ways of being together.

Giles made short work of the small, decorative buttons down her back. He slipped the gown down her arms, taking the opportunity to kiss her slight shoulders, the tops of her arms. She smelled divine, of flowers and a unique scent that was wholly Sarah.

Goose bumps rose on her skin, and he quickly pulled at the ties of her corset. Undressing Sarah was akin to unwrapping a gift. Having Sarah, such as she now was, willing in his arms and his, was the best Yuletide present he could have possessed. Her gown pooled at her waist, and Giles ripped her shift over her head, her corset next, discarding it somewhere about the foot of the bed.

She stood, and her dress fell to the floor. Giles took her into his arms, tumbling them down onto the soft linen. They bounced, and she chuckled, the throaty tenor of her voice hardened his cock.

He pulled back to admire the view of her before him. Her cheeks were flushed, her breasts full and heavy, all but begged for his touch. His mouth watered and, unable to deny himself a moment longer, he gave in to the desire thrumming through his blood like a raging torrent.

Giles licked her beaded nipple before taking her into his mouth. She moaned, her fingers spiking into his hair, and he kissed and paid homage to her breast while his other hand kneaded and teased the other.

"Oh, yes," she sighed. "You have no notion of how long I've wanted you this way."

He inwardly cursed all the missed opportunities, the years they were not together so. He'd wanted Sarah for as long as he could remember, and from this day forward, he would not be separated from her again.

Nothing would deny him her hand.

"Marry me." Giles kissed his way down her chest to her stomach, paying homage to the little freckle that sat beside her naval. He went farther, running his hand down the inside of her leg before touching the wet heat between her thighs.

He felt her start at his touch, and he looked up along her body, meeting the question in her hooded gaze.

"Lie back. I want to show you what we can have."

She bit her lip, sending desire straight to his cock. He pushed down his own needs, promising himself his turn would come. Soon, she would be his, and they would be one.

Giles kissed the inside of her thigh, breathing deep the sweet, musky scent of her mons. She undulated beneath him, and he held her legs apart, wanting to see her wet, pink lips that were his to enjoy.

He licked her swollen nubbin, and she gasped, her hands no longer pushing at his shoulders, but wrapping into his hair, holding him in place.

A dark, hungry need tore through him. He licked along her cunny, kissing and lathing her honeyed flesh to a fever. He made sure to stroke and frustrate her nubbin, running his thumb between her lips and tantalizing her where they would soon be joined.

She mewled, gasping with each of his tongue's strokes. His balls tightened, his cock heavy and erect, his release taunting deep in his gut.

"Yes, Giles. Ohhh, please, more."

He'd give her as much as she liked. He slipped one finger into her scorching heat. Her body tightened, contracted about him, and it took all of his self-control not to wrench up, placing his aching cock at her entrance and take her.

Soon. Soon, they would be one.

She lifted her bottom off the bed, undulating against his mouth, and he knew she was close. Without fear or shame, she rode his face, took pleasure from him, and never would his life be the same.

He would marry the woman beneath him. From this day forward, he could not live without her. How he had survived all the years was beyond him.

He kissed her fully, lathing her to a writhing frenzied, begging lover before he suckled on her clitoris, and she gasped, moaning as her release spiraled through her.

An overwhelming sense of power thrummed through his veins as he milked her of her pleasure. With ragged breath, and only when he was sure she was satisfied, did he move.

He came up over her, wrapping her legs about his hips. She watched him, her eyes pools of satiated desire and expectation. A small quirk tilted her lips. He placed himself at her entrance, meeting her eyes.

Sarah reached up, wrapping her arms about his neck, and he thrust into her, taking her virginity, and finally, they were one.

Lady Sarah Farley was his.

Sarah had thought Giles taking her would hurt. How very wrong she was. After his wickedly clever mouth had brought her to such pleasure that even now she could not catch her breath, his intrusion into her body only brought more pleasure.

With each thrust, it teased, thrummed, and reignited the climax she had just experienced.

She wanted him deeper, harder, faster. With a wantonness that she did not know she possessed, she spread her legs wider, hooked them higher on his back, and gave herself over to him.

To pleasure.

"Sarah," he gasped against her lips. "I've wanted you for so long."

"And I you." She held him against her, needing him to take her. To give her the soul-shattering pleasure he'd just bestowed. Once would never be enough. She needed more. Now.

"Take me," she panted. He did not disappoint. He thrust hard and deep. The sound of their flesh meeting, of creating pleasure echoed throughout the room and was music to her ears.

He kissed her, and she took the opportunity to run her hands down his back. Sweat-slicked skin met her fingers as she ran them down the taut, flexing muscles beside his spine. His bottom thrust against her and she clasped him there, enjoying the feel of him within her, taking her.

She would never get enough of this man.

The pleasure his mouth wrought teased her yet again, and she rose to meet his every move, and then she was there, spiraling out of control. Pleasure rocked through her, more pronounced, coarser, and overwhelming her soul.

"Giles," she cried.

He moaned, taking her, their bodies a burst of needs and wants, of receiving and giving.

"Sarah," he panted against her lips, kissing her softly. "Please tell me you will marry me now?"

She grinned, snuggling into the crook of his arm when he rolled to his side, pulling her up against him. She lay one leg over him, idly playing with his chest, which rose and fell in quick pants.

"Yes," she said, looking up and meeting his gaze. "I will marry you." And finally, he would be hers. Always.

CHAPTER 12

Sarah stuck her head out into the darkened passage just before dawn, glancing up and down to ensure no one was about. The servants would be up soon, and if she were to sneak back to her bedroom without being seen, now was her chance.

She turned, taking one last glimpse of Giles as he slept in the bed they'd shared. He lay on his back, his arm sprawled out over her pillow where she'd rested. Her heart fluttered in her chest, and regretfully, she turned, slipping into the hall and closing the door behind her, taking care not to make any loud noises.

"Good morning, sister."

Sarah squealed, slapping a hand over her mouth before she woke any of the other guests. Footsteps sounded in the room she'd just emerged from, and the door wrenched open.

Giles stood at the threshold, hastily tied breeches his only attire, his chest, one she'd never tire of looking upon flexing with each breath. The moonlight from the window at the end of the hall, the only illuminating light.

"What is wrong?" Giles's words faded at the sight of Hugh glaring at them both.

Her brother pushed Sarah out the way and, with a sickening crunch, his fist connected with Giles's nose.

Sarah gasped, watched as Giles flayed backward before he fell with a crashing thud on the floor. Sarah kneeled at Giles' side, checking him as best she could. He pinched the bridge of his nose, blood seeped between his fingers and onto his lips, staining his teeth. He held up a hand, stilling her brother from doing any more damage.

"I suppose I deserved your wrath, but I'll not be hit a second time," Giles said, letting Sarah help him to stand.

Hugh shut the door to the bedroom, enclosing all three of them in the room. "What the hell do you think you're doing with my sister?"

Hugh glared at them both, his eyes wild with temper. Never had Sarah seen Hugh so incensed and shame threaded through her that she'd caused him such distress. If this were to get out to the other guests what she had done with Giles, the scandal would be all the *ton* would talk of next Season. Marriage or not.

That Hugh had asked her not to cause a scandal was the veriest dishonor.

"I asked Sarah to marry me, and she has agreed. I would never touch her had she said no."

Sarah raised her brow, unsure that was true. She was certain that if she wished it, she could have seduced Giles before last night.

"Is this true, Sarah?" her brother asked, pinning her to her spot, the anger and disappointment shimmering in his eyes, eliminating any ire she felt at being caught. At receiving a thorough set down from her brother over her conduct.

"Giles has asked for me to be his wife, and I want that in return." She met Giles's gaze, her heart taking a little leap at the warmth and adoration she read in his blue orbs.

"How long have you been behaving in this manner?" Her brother shook his head. "I should have guessed yesterday when I caught you both upstairs, looking as guilty as you do now."

"Excuse me, Hugh, but I'm not a child. I'm eight and twenty and quite capable of making my own decisions."

Her brother pointed his finger at her nose. "You can make decisions, Sarah, but this one is what I specifically asked you not to."

"No one needs to know. You're the only person who has seen me this morning. If we leave now, announce the betrothal in the morning, all will be well."

Hugh glared at them both, his balled fists flexing at his sides. "I ought to call you out, Gordan." His jaw clenched, and he took a deep breath. "But I suppose since you're to be my brother-in-law by choice not by my decree, I shall let you live."

Sarah sighed, and Giles reached over to take her hand. She stared at the blood that marked his chest and face. Sarah moved over to the pitcher of water and bowl in his room, poured some water and rinsed out a washcloth.

"Here," she said, handing it to Giles. He gave her his thanks and set it against his nose, wincing a little as he did so.

"I'm sorry you had to find out about Sarah and me in this way, Hugh, but I love her. I want her to be my wife. I promise that later today, I was coming to ask you for your permission to make her my wife."

Hugh rubbed a hand through his hair, the dark circles under his eyes telling Sarah her brother was weary.

"We are sorry, Hugh. Please don't be angry. I want this time to be a happy one." It had been so very long since she'd been so content.

He stared at them both without a word before he nodded, once. "Very well. I give you my consent, and I do wish you both very happy. You can be married as soon as we can gain a special license." Her brother met her gaze, some of the anger dispelling from his dark orbs. "Congratulations, Sarah."

She went into his arms, holding him tight. "Thank you, Hugh, for being so understanding."

"Yes, well," he said, relenting and pulling her tight in his arms. "You may not have gone about this the way that I asked, but it is done now. All will be well, I'm sure." He set her back and started for the door. He paused, turning to watch them both. "Come, Sarah. I will escort you to your room."

Sarah met Giles's eyes, and he nodded, winking at her. She smiled, bidding him goodbye, her words but a whisper, and followed her brother from the room.

He didn't say anything to her as they made their way back to her room. He opened her bedroom door, pushing it wide. "In you go, dear sister. Do not let me catch you out and about the house again. Not until you're a married woman. Do I make myself clear?"

She swallowed her retort, wanting to remind him that he wasn't so very well-behaved when Molly was in Rome. Sarah was privy to how they came together, so her brother's high-handedness was a little galling.

Even so, she would do as he bade because, in the end, she would marry Giles. The sacrifice would be worth the wait. "Perfectly clear, brother. I shall do as you ask."

He watched until the door to her room closed. Once

more alone, she ran over to her bed, slipping under the soft sheets and heavy blankets. She smiled, contentment thrumming through her veins. She was engaged to Giles, Marquess Gordan. Excitement somersaulted her stomach, and the day could not start soon enough. She wanted to shout it from the rooftops that they would be married. Her husband and she his wife.

How well that sounded to her ears. A dream that finally came true.

CHAPTER 13

Before dinner the same day, Sarah sat beside Giles in the drawing room, an overwhelming sense of happiness consuming her as her brother announced that she and Giles were engaged.

Congratulations sounded loud in the room. An array of guests came up to them to wish them very happy.

Sarah laughed, thanked each one in turn. Giles pulled her into his side, watching her with an expression that made her stomach twist into delicious knots. "I hope you're happy, my lady?" he asked, his eyes dark pools of an emotion she hoped would be voiced again soon. She wanted to hear him say that he loved her as much as she had always loved him.

"So happy," she said, meaning it more than anything she'd ever said before in her life.

Dinner that evening was a boisterous, excitable evening. Everyone seemed to be in a rush to speak, drink wine, celebrate the Christmas season, and Sarah and Giles's betrothal, which only added to the celebrations.

The after-dinner drinks were no different. Sarah sat on a settee watching as Molly and Hugh toasted her and Giles yet again, her brother's wide smile and laughing eyes telling all in attendance how very pleased he was for his sister. Even if this morning, he'd been so very mad.

Sarah caught the eye of Lady Rackliffe, who excused herself from her small social circle and strolled over to Sarah.

The forthcoming conversation, as awkward as it would be, had to be had. Lady Rackliffe was, after all, once betrothed to Giles. No doubt, the woman would, at the very least, have to remind Sarah that she was asked first, no matter what the outcome had been for them both.

"Lady Sarah, may I say how very happy I am for you and Lord Gordan? You shall be very happy, I'm sure," she said, sitting next to her and sipping her wine.

"Thank you, my lady. That is very kind of you to say." Sarah almost rolled her eyes at the banality of their conversation. Even so, she did not wish to extend their little tête-a-tête any more than she had to. They had never been friends in the past. Certainly, Lady Rackliffe thought herself above most within society, even within her own circle of friends.

"I must say the news of your betrothal to Giles has shocked me. I did not even know there was anything representing affection between you both. From knowing Giles all these years, how he lived his life in London, I'm surprised you accepted him so quickly."

Sarah stiffened her back, refusing to let this woman's words deflate her agreeable mood. "Lord Gordan," she said, reminding Lady Rackliffe that she no longer had the right to use his given name. She threw that away the moment she threw his lordship over for Lord Rackliffe. "He is an honorable man. I have little concern about his life before me. I think him the best of men and one who'll make me extremely happy."

The idea of days and nights in his company, to wake up in his arms, have his children, sent a thrill through her she'd not felt since the moment she closed the space between them and kissed him on a moonlit terrace in London ten years before.

Lady Rackliffe's mouth pinched into a displeased line. "Oh, I'm sure he will not stray, my dear. But," she said, biting her lip, "it does seem odd that his morals would allow this change of heart. You know why, do you not, he never offered for your hand during your first Season. Why no one offered."

Sarah was not sure she wanted to know, certainly not from this viperous, gossiping snake.

"I do not know, no." Nor did she wish to be privy to the details. What was in the past as far as she was concerned needed to stay there. If she were to endure the *ton* and re-enter society, she had to be able to let go of their wrong-doing to her brother and move forward without hate in her heart.

Lady Rackliffe chuckled a high-pitched cackle that made her ears hurt. "The scandal, of course," she whis-pered, making sure no one else could hear. "Giles's father was friends with your late mama. He did not approve of the scandal Lord Hugh had bestowed on the family. Of course, even knowing the truth as we do now that it was the duke, and oldest brother Henry who was at fault, the late Lord Gordan did not know that.

“He saw his good friend, the duchess heartbroken that

her son had acted in such a way and refused to counter a friendship between Giles and Hugh. Had demanded Giles remove himself from your family and cease all contact. Of course, he did. Giles was always a good son to his parents. He set off to London, courted me, and asked for my hand before the first week of the Season had ended."

Sarah swallowed past the lump in her throat at Lady Rackliffe's words. Was this true? Had Giles thrown them aside like trash to appease his father? She took a sip of wine, needing at that very moment more fortification than this. A hard whiskey or brandy would do very well to dull the ache in her chest.

"You are mistaken, my lady. Giles would not have forgone a lifelong friendship with my family regarding a scandal that was of the duke's making."

Lady Rackliffe shrugged, smirking. "Well, did he visit Lord Farley when he lived in Rome? Did Lord Gordan travel down to Kent and visit you here at the Abbey? I think the fact that he did not is proof enough, no?"

Sarah fought to breathe. She looked up and met the contemplative stare of Giles. Not wanting to confront him here, she threw him a wobbly smile. He grinned back at her, and her heart broke in her chest.

He'd believed the lie? Had towed his father's line and thrown them out with the scandal. Had ceased his friendship with Hugh and her due to not wishing to dirty his name by the association.

How could he have done such a thing? She and Hugh were innocent of the crime. Certainly, she had nothing to do with what her mother and elder brother had concocted to hide.

All the years she never saw or heard from him came rushing back, the pain his absence had caused in her heart.

The past week with him here at the Abbey, she had allowed him to make her forget his wrongdoing.

She was a fool to have let his pretty face and words trick her into disregarding the truth that now having been told was blatantly obvious.

"Lord Gordan was busy elsewhere, that is all." It was all Sarah could say in defense of Lady Rackliffe's words. What else could she say at hearing such a devastating truth about the man she had agreed to marry?

"I know that you held a tendre for Giles during our first Season, and you must know that I did not mean to steal him from you. Our family was not going through a troubled time as your own, and the late marquess thought I was the better match for Giles. He agreed, of course, and offered for my hand. I hope you weren't too heartbroken, my dear, for look at you now. You have won him in the end."

Lady Rackliffe's tone was lathed with sarcasm and hate, each word dripping with scorn. Sarah met her ladyship's gaze, her own narrowing in inspection.

"Which begs the question as to why you would throw him over for the ancient and decrepit Lord Rackliffe? I know that if I had the choice between Lord Gordan and Lord Rackliffe, I certainly would not have picked a gentleman who was old enough to be my great grandfather." Sarah downed her wine in one swallow. "You must have loved him a great deal to have married a gentleman fifty years your senior." Sarah waved her empty crystal glass before Lady Rackliffe's face. "If you'll excuse me, I need another glass of wine. A lot more celebrating to be had."

Sarah stood and, without a backward glance at the

gaping Lady Rackliffe, joined Giles, who was speaking to the Duke and Duchess of Whitstone.

Tonight was not the time, Sarah reminded herself. Later, she would sneak to Giles's room and ask him the truth. Only then would she know what she would do and what her future would encompass.

CHAPTER 14

Sarah paced her bedroom late that evening, the skirts of her pink silk shift and dressing gown billowing about her legs. The house the past hour had been quiet. Was Giles in his room? Or was he still downstairs with her brother and celebrating the impending wedding? An event that she was not certain would take place, not now that she knew why he'd abandoned them all those years ago.

A light scratch sounded on her door, and her pacing ceased. She flew to the door, cracking it open a little to see who was there. Giles's handsome, smiling visage greeted her, and she stepped back, letting him in. He smiled at her, reaching for her the moment she shut and locked the door. Sarah stepped back, holding up her hand. "We need to talk. Before anything else is settled between us."

He frowned, his face a mask of confusion. "Very well. What is it that you wish to discuss?"

Sarah walked over to the settee before her fire and sat. Giles joined her, taking her hand. She didn't pull away as she should. Instead, she allowed the small gesture, if only to will herself to what she must ask.

"I spoke with Lady Rackliffe tonight, and she explained your betrothal to her with a little more clarity."

"Really." His brows drew farther together still, his eyes narrowing. "What did she say?"

"Did you push me away the night I kissed you because of the scandal that was ripping my family apart?"

He ran a hand over his jaw, and Sarah could see he was choosing his words carefully. An inkling of fear rippled through her. So there was truth to Lady Rackliffe's words.

"When you kissed me, I wasn't prepared for what that kiss would mean."

Sarah frowned, knowing only too well what that kiss meant to her at least. It had changed her world, made her realize to the very core of her soul that she wanted him, and no one else. For all the years she'd pined for him, longed for him to look her way had not been an impossible dream. Had it meant anything to Giles? Or had she been nothing but an annoyance, a walking scandal that he did not want to be associated with?

"What do you even mean by that?"

He gestured between them. "Your kiss unraveled the world that I convinced myself I wanted. I was betrothed to Edith for only one day and could not cry off. I was trapped, furious at myself that I had chosen the wrong woman."

She met his gaze, wishing that were true, but it was not all of his truth. There were parts of his story he was keeping from her. "Did your father command you cease your friendship with our family over what Hugh was accused of? Even though you of all people, one of our closest friends, should have known Hugh could not be guilty of such a crime."

He was silent a moment, a muscle working in his jaw. He stood, striding to the mantel, leaning on it as he considered the roaring flames in the hearth. "My father was not an easy man, Sarah. Certainly was not one whom a son would go up against." He turned, meeting her gaze, and the fear that lurked in his eyes made her stomach churn. She hated to see him so fearful of the truth. Only someone guilty of the crime, understood the ramifications, would be troubled. "My father demanded me to marry Edith, or he would cut me off. Leave me to rot, I believe, were his words."

"Your father was my mother's friend for years. How could he hate her son so much as to demand this of you?" To be so cruel did not make sense. The late marquess could not have been so blind and wicked.

"They remained friends, even though he ensured the association did not sully his son and only heir. When Edith did not show up at the church for our wedding, my father's fight to tell me what to do seemed to dissipate from that point onward. He became an old man overnight, and within three years was gone."

"What about all the other years you stayed away?" She shook her head, fisting her hands in her lap. "Why? If I meant so very much to you, why did you let me rot in Kent? Left me under the protection of a brother who gave no security at all."

"I thought you shunned me. I did not think that you wanted anything further to do with me after the way I treated you after our kiss."

"I did not like you at all, that is true, but if you came to me then, explained why you had acted as you did, it would not have been so bad, but now..." Sarah stood, coming before him. "I could not have meant any great deal to you if you stayed away. You believed the scandal, didn't you? You knew Henry was a rogue, hell-bent on causing and living a debauched life, and still, you believed Hugh was guilty of the crime against Miss Cox."

"I did not believe that of Hugh. Never." He clasped her hands, squeezing them. "Please, Sarah, you must understand."

"No, I do not need to understand anything. I do not need to believe you at all." She tore her hands away, putting distance between them. "You lied to me, and worse is that your ex-betrothed threw the truth in my face." How many others in the *ton* would laugh at her for being so blind? Had Lady Rackliffe told her knowledge regarding Giles and Sarah to everyone at the house party? Were they laughing at her behind her back?

Humiliation tore through her and anger thrummed in her veins that the *ton* was once again laughing at her family. Snickering and speaking about them behind their backs.

He stared down at her, a shadow crossing his eyes. "I did not tell Lady Rackliffe anything. If she knew anything at all, it was at my father's doing."

"You've made a fool of me, Giles, and I won't stand for it. I promised myself years ago that I would never allow the *ton* to laugh and criticize my family. I have not, to this day, missed the society that I once graced. I cannot marry a man who believed Hugh was guilty. A man who allowed his father to dictate whom he should marry all because of a lie. Did you try to contact Hugh at all when he was in Rome?"

Giles dropped his hands at his sides, his face paling. "I did not."

Sarah shook her head, not believing what she was hearing. How had she not seen the reason why Giles had cut them off? It was not simply because she'd thrown herself at him, and he did not feel the same way. It was because he'd been told to stay away, to remove his oldest friends from his life. Do as he was told or else.

"I cannot marry you, Giles."

Sarah started for the door, needing him to leave. A hand clamped about her arm, wrenching her back. "You're crying off from our understanding? Even though I love you as much as you love me?"

His declaration sent a frisson of pleasure to course through her, but she pushed it down, stomped on it until it was no more. Her heart ached in her chest, her throat tight with unshed tears. She would not give in to emotion. She'd learned a long time ago to remain calm, don't show a response to situations that could cause her pain or give others power over her. "I will not marry a man who treated my family so poorly. Did you know how I suffered here in England without Hugh? Without you?"

The pitying look he bestowed on her fired her temper. She paced before him, her mind a whirlwind of thoughts. "Henry was awful after he schemed his way out of ruining Miss Cox. He threw parties here, lived for nothing but debauchery and strife. I had no one. Society shunned me, so I stayed here, hiding like some felon who had committed a crime. His friends would come from town, the gentleman I had danced with during my first Season. I soon learned to be wary. They were wont to follow Henry's etiquette. Whenever my brother came to stay, I fled to the dowager house."

He took a step toward her, and she put out her hand, stopping him. "I do not need your comfort."

"I did not know, Sarah. I would have come had I known. I'm sorry."

"Everyone knew what Henry was like, you more than anyone else, but you chose to stay away. I was not important enough to you that you would come and visit like you had when we were younger. I allowed myself to be swept up in your attention to me the past week. Allowed your sweet words and even sweeter kisses to taint my recollection of the past. How fortunate Lady Rackliffe reminded me of my failing."

A muscle worked in his jaw, and she looked toward the fire, not wanting to see the sheen of unshed tears in his eyes. "I made a mistake, do not punish us both for the rest of our lives by doing this, Sarah."

"Leave," she said, her voice cold and emotionless, just as her soul was right at this very moment. He'd left her before. Surely she would survive if he left her again.

"This is a mistake." Giles started for the door, pausing at her side a moment. Sarah willed him to leave. To go now. If he stopped, if he pulled her into his arms, she wasn't certain she would be so strong to deny him.

Sarah did not respond, merely listened as her door opened and closed quietly behind the one man in the world she did love and who, for the second time in her short life, had broken her heart.

CHAPTER 15

The following morning Giles waited in the Duke of St. Albans' study, needing to speak to him before the day commenced. His gut churned, his eyes itched with a lack of sleep. Would Hugh aid him in winning Sarah back, or tell him to bugger off after hearing why he'd distanced himself for so many years from Hugh's family?

The duke strode into the room, his steps slowing when he saw him seated before his desk. "Gordan?" He came the rest of the way into the room, slipping his tall frame into his leather-back chair. "To what do I owe the pleasure?" His Grace asked, smiling.

Giles wondered how long the comradeship would last, considering he'd lied to the duke's sister, and Hugh also. Giles could only hope his old school friend would let the past be. They had all made mistakes, granted this was one of the biggest that Giles had made. And one he wanted to right before he lost the only woman he'd ever loved.

Something about the knowing depths of the duke's

gaze told him he may have already heard why he wished to see him this morning.

"St. Albans," he said, nodding in welcome. "I need to speak to you quite urgently. It's important."

"I believe it is." His Grace narrowed his eyes, leaning back in his chair. "Sarah did not appear to be the incandescent happy bride of the evening before at breakfast. Have you quarreled?"

Giles cleared his throat. *You could say that.* "Sarah no longer wishes to marry me, and after what I'm about to tell you, I would not be surprised if you wish for me to leave the Christmas festivities."

The duke raised his brow, throwing him a contemplative inspection. "Well, that does sound ominous. What happened?" he asked.

Giles told him of his engagement to Edith. How the union came about at the behest of his father. How his father had wanted to distance his only son and heir from Hugh, his closest friend after the scandal, citing bad influence and being tainted by association. The kiss Sarah bestowed on him at a London ball and his reaction to the said kiss. He told Hugh all of his shame, his regrets, and mistakes.

A muscle worked on Hugh's jaw, his eyes narrowed, but he didn't utter a word. Giles met Hugh's eyes, hard, dark pools he could not read, and he waited for the demand to leave to be spoken. For him to declare he ought to let Sarah go and find another woman to marry.

Instead, the reaction Hugh gave him was not the one he expected.

He laughed. So hard, in fact, his eyes watered.

"Well, you have made a mess of things, have you not?" Hugh stood, striding over to a decanter of whiskey, pouring two good portions into crystal glasses. He came over to him, handing him one. "Drink. If you are to win my sister back, you'll need your fortification."

Giles did as Hugh bade him, the burn of the amber liquid down his throat reminding him he was alive and being so, there was the opportunity, the possibility, to win Sarah back.

"You're not angry?" Giles asked, unsure how he could not be so. "I ceased a lifetime of friendship simply due to what my father and the *ton* believed to be true. I should not have. I knew you better than anyone, I should have guessed that Henry was behind your downfall."

Hugh waved his concerns aside. "Henry and my mother were to blame. Not you. Nor are you responsible for your father's reaction to the scandal that rocked my family. Sarah should understand this."

Giles had hoped that she would, but it was not so. "I should not have allowed my father to dictate my life. I lied to her, and she knows that I did. In her opinion, I chose to follow the *ton*, let their response, and opinions guide me away from my friendship with you both. I did not go to her after my father's death as I should have. She cannot forgive me."

Hugh sighed, leaning forward and crossing his hands on the desk. "Why did you not repair the friendship after the marquess's death?"

Giles cringed, wishing he had. "I had not seen Sarah for some years by then, and our parting did not give me the sense that she wished to know if I were alive or dead."

Disappointment lurked in Hugh's gaze, and Giles knew that particular point was his downfall. Why he could lose her. He should have gone to her immediately. Begged for forgiveness and made her remember how very much they liked each other. "I know," he groaned. "You do not have to say it. I know I buggered up."

Hugh nodded. "On that point, yes, you did, but we've all made mistakes. I more than most. I should not have allowed my family to push me from the only home I had, and yet I did. I took their financial support, moved to Rome, and started a new life. All the while, I let an innocent woman suffer in England at the hands of my brother's treatment."

Giles did not know what to say to such a declaration. Since Hugh's return, they had not discussed the scandal or outcomes of the time but had been happy to put it all behind them. Move forward, pick up the friendship where they once were, and forget the duke's brother and his mistreatment of those he was supposed to love.

"Sarah dislikes the *ton* and their treatment of her and me. While I understand why she's reacted in such a way, I also know that she will be thinking clearer in a couple of days. Do not give up on her, Giles. I've known that since we were boys on the brink of becoming men, there was a special bond between you two. I would like nothing more than to welcome you into our family, to become my brother. I always saw you like one, more than the actual blood brother I was saddled with."

Giles took a calming breath. The duke's comforting words went a long way in dispelling the gnawing worry he'd been plagued with ever since Sarah told him their understanding was no more.

"She does not want to marry me. How do I win her back? I have waited years to be with her. I cannot lose her now."

Hugh threw him a pitying look. Giles knew he was pitiful at this very moment, but panic threatened to seize him at the mere thought of walking away. Of hearing months or years from now that Sarah had married another. Loved another. He would not let it happen. She loved him, not anyone else. He simply had to remind her of that fact.

"Let me talk to her, Giles. As her brother and the one person she trusts most in the world, let me see if I can get her to see another point of view."

While Giles doubted it would be successful, he would try anything not to lose her. "Thank you, Hugh. I cannot thank you enough for this kindness."

Hugh stood, coming around the desk to clasp his shoulder. "While I cannot promise success, I will do all that I can. As you know, my sister can be quite stubborn with independent thought, that is hard to sway at times."

Giles chuckled, knowing how true that was. It was one of the reasons he loved her as much as he did. She was no wilting flower, his love. "She is a rare beauty." And he would win her back, losing her simply was not an option.

CHAPTER 16

Sarah sat in the duke and duchess's private parlor, not for use by the other guests at the house party. She sat on the settee facing the fire, waiting for her family to join her.

She had requested they come to see her, to hear of her change of circumstance, where it regarded Giles.

The thought of him made her skin chill, and she rubbed her arms, pulling the woolen shawl about her shoulders, her light-green gown not warm enough on this cold day.

She had not seen him at breakfast this morning, had not reveled in his company, his wicked glances across the table and lively conversation.

How could he have pushed her away and discarded her when she needed him the most? His actions were unforgivable.

Molly and Hugh strode into the room. Molly came over to her, kissing her cheeks in turn, before sitting beside her. Hugh stood before the fire, warming his hands.

"Sarah, I must say that I'm pleased you asked to speak to me, for there is a matter we need to discuss."

"There is? What was it that you wanted to talk to me about?" She had not mentioned anything to anyone about her and Giles's parting ways. Had she been too sharp with one of the guests? Lady Rackliffe, perhaps, who had a way of getting under her skin.

Hugh turned, facing them, his hands clasped behind his back. Molly took Sarah's hand, giving it a comforting squeeze. "What is wrong? You're both starting to frighten me."

"Be assured there is nothing wrong, but I have spoken to Giles this morning. He has told me everything that happened between you."

Molly threw her a look full of pity, and Sarah sighed. Not wanting anyone to pity her for standing up for what she believed. If Giles truly loved her, he would have fought for her. Came to her the moment his father had passed. He did not.

"No matter what your choice, we're here for you, Sarah."

Sarah thanked her kind sister-in-law, but turned back to her brother. "He spoke to you? I hope you made it clear that his actions toward you and our family were unacceptable. Hurtful and not those of a friend. Which, I had to remind him of the fact, he was supposed to be."

Her brother's lips thinned into a displeased line. "Come, Sarah, you know it is not always as easy as that. I am proof of such, am I not? What mother and Henry forced me into was perhaps a time when I should have shown the remnants of a backbone, but I did not. An act that I will forever regret, but one that I did to save what little was left of my life. Giles kept his distance as per his father's decree. Such action may well be displeasing. It is hard to deny one's sire when they threaten you."

"He's an only child, Hugh. He could have refused, and there would be nothing the late marquess could have done. He may have lost the access to funds, but what is that when you have stood by your morals? Your friends?" *People who loved you.*

"That is unfair, Sarah. Not everything is so black and white. There are portions of gray in life."

"If he liked us so very much, why did he not come to see me after his father had passed? Why wait until you returned from Rome? Why not write to you and keep your friendship a secret?"

"You know why, he told you himself. While we men may pine for a woman who has captured our heart, realize that we're only living a half life when we're not with those we love," Hugh said, looking to Molly, his face softening with affection for his wife. "It does not mean we do not have pride. And Giles did write to me, Whitstone too. They never abandoned me to my exile completely." Hugh paused, a frown between his brow. "Can you remember the last words you spoke to Giles on the night you kissed him at the London ball?"

Sarah gasped, heat blooming on her cheeks at the fact that her brother knew of her kissing Giles and their following argument.

She thought back to that night. She could still smell the freshly cut grass, the flowering roses, and the ivy prickle against her back as she tried to hide in the greenery.

"I told him I did not wish to see him again. That our friendship was at an end, and nothing would persuade me to think otherwise on the matter." She swallowed the lump that wedged in her throat. Giles had looked devastated at her words, as if she had ripped his heart out and thrown it into the gardens.

"How can you stand it, Hugh, what the *ton* did to us, not Henry and Mama, but you and me? We're the ones who paid the price for their deception other than Miss Cox," she said, whispering sorry to Molly, who was the young woman's cousin. "They shunned us, talked about us, and did not hide the fact that we had fallen from a great social height. I do not care what they thought. I do not. I could let the *ton* go hang and not glance back, but Hugh, Giles was one of those whispers. He agreed with their views, left us alone and without friends. How can you forgive that? How do you expect me to marry such a man?"

Hugh came and sat beside her, taking her other hand. "He never spoke of us. I'm certain of that. He merely went about his own business and got on with things without us to keep his father happy. I suppose when the marquess passed, Giles thought too much time had gone by for there ever to be forgiveness between you and him. But there can be. You can be happy, Sarah, if you let the past go. Truly let it go and stop it from festering inside of you." Hugh winked at Molly, and out of Sarah's peripheral eye, she could see her sister-in-law grinning. "You can love and live as you've only dreamed. I want that for you too. You're my sister, let us not let Henry and Mama ruin our future and our past. They do not deserve the power."

Sarah sniffed, swiping her damp cheeks at her brother's wise words.

Could she forgive Giles? Did she want to have a future with him after knowing all that she did? Sarah only had to think about that fact a moment or two before realizing the truth. Yes, of course, she did. She wanted him in all ways, even if he had acted a total fool and almost lost her forever.

She stood, striding for the door.

"Where are you going?" Molly asked, standing.

Sarah wrenched the door open and stopped, turning to face her family. "To catch myself a marquess before he does something foolish once more, like ask Lady Rackliffe for her hand again, and I lose him forever."

Hugh chuckled, pulling Molly down beside him. "Close the door on your way out, sister."

Sarah rolled her eyes at her brother's wickedness with his wife, only too glad not to be privy to their love. They were worse than anyone she'd ever met, and she too wanted the same.

With Giles.

CHAPTER 17

Giles stood looking out his bedroom window, watching as the carriage came around from the stable. Behind him, his valet packed his belongings in his trunks. A maid came out from the house's front door, handing warming bricks to his driver, who placed them on the carriage floor.

It would be a cold trip back to London, but it was one he must take. He could not stay here any longer, not with Sarah wishing for him to leave.

He clutched the back of his neck, rolling his shoulders to dispel the tension that plagued him after their last words. He had tried to make her see his position, right or wrong, he had obeyed his sire and, to his detriment, had lost Sarah in the process.

That they could be together now caused frustration and impatience to run through his veins. If only she put the past behind her, stopped allowing others' actions to guide their lives, they could be happy together. Have a life, a marriage.

"Excuse me, my lord. We're all packed. I shall have the trunks carried down and will meet you at the carriage."

"Thank you, John," Giles said, turning from the window, unwilling to leave the Abbey without one last chance of winning Sarah's trust and love.

He beat his valet out of the room, striding toward Sarah's bedroom door when he spotted her all but running down the corridor. His steps slowed, and he schooled his features, unsure of what, if anything, seeing her running in the direction of his room meant.

He stopped, bowed. "Lady Sarah." His eyes devoured every morsel of her, her fitting, complementary gown that showed off her figure to its full advantage. A body he had savored, enjoyed, and worshiped only two nights before. The light-green muslin with pretty darker-green flowers embroidered on it, making her eyes seem fiercely olive.

"Giles," she breathed, fighting to catch her breath.

That she used his given name and not his title sent a frisson of hope to course through his blood. Had she changed her mind? Had Hugh talked her 'round to forgive him? Or was she merely coming to ensure he did, in fact, leave?

Two footmen entered his room behind him, and within a moment, walked out into the passage, carrying one of his trunks.

Her face fell, along with her shoulders. "You're leaving?"

He nodded. "I think it is best, yes."

She watched him a moment, and he could see she was choosing her words carefully. He wanted to take her into his arms, pull her close, and tell her that he was sorry. That he'd never meant to hurt her. That he was simply obeying a father that he never wished to disappoint.

Sarah clamped her hands before her, raising her chin. "We need to talk." She clasped his hand, pulling him down the hall and toward where the picture gallery ran. He'd not been in this part of the house for many years, and following Sarah as quick as he was, didn't allow him to take in the most recent painting of her that Hugh had commissioned.

They stopped at the end of the long hall, the bank of windows overlooking the side of the house's gardens, allowing light to flood the space.

Giles looked back to where they had come from and noted how very alone they were in this part of the house.

"I do not want you to leave, Giles." She stepped against him until the hem of her gown slipped across his hessian boots. "I was wrong to judge you as harshly as I did. While I will not forget or forgive what society did to my brother and myself, I will forgive you. I love you, and I'm sorry for blaming you for all my anger. I will never do so again."

Giles reached for her, pulling her against him, breathing deep the sweet smell of berries from her hair. "You have nothing to apologize for. I'm the one who is sorry, Sarah. I should have declared to my father that I would be friends and love whomever I pleased. Love whomever I wanted. It was one of the reasons why I was so angry with you the night you kissed me. I knew the moment I had you in my arms that we would never be. That through my foolishness, allowing others to dictate my actions and life that the one woman I did want beside me for the rest of my life would not be you. I had offered to Edith, and it was too late. I lashed out, blamed you for my own failings. Please forgive me."

Sarah reached up, running her hands over his jaw. Her eyes shimmered with unshed tears, and he wiped them away with his thumbs when they fell. "No tears. No more looking back. Walk beside me now, into our future. Will you marry me, please? I cannot live another day without you in my life." Never had he ever said anything so true or had wanted anything so desperately in his life.

She was his everything, and from this day forward, if she said yes, his sole purpose in life was making her incandescently happy.

"I will marry you, yes. Now please tell me you will stay. I cannot be without a dance partner for the Christmas ball."

"Wild horses could not drag me away from you." Giles leaned down, stealing a kiss, reveling in the feel of her again in his arms.

He did not let her go for a very long time...

EPILOGUE

They were married Christmas morning under a steady fall of snow. The small church that sat on the St. Albans estate was full of local gentry and those who stayed at the Abbey for the Christmas festivities. The ball that night a time to celebrate the nuptials of Sarah and Giles and Yuletide.

She stood beside Giles, her arm wrapped about his as they watched some of the guests take part in a waltz.

Warmth blossomed in her chest, and Sarah was sure her heart might burst with happiness at being married to her one and only love. She glanced up at him, caught him watching her, and her stomach flipped deliciously.

"You look like you're scheming something, my lord."

He chuckled, a deep rumble that spiked her need of him. It had been so very long since they had come together, Giles wishing to wait until they were married, and Sarah had to admit she was well past ready to have him in her bed once again.

"I'm simply happy." He paused, leaning down to

whisper in her ear, "And looking forward to having you in my bed this evening."

Heat bloomed on her cheeks, and she could not stop a grin from forming on her lips. "Maybe we could slip away? No one will pay any heed to us, leaving early. I should think it would be expected."

A wicked light entered his eye, and he took her hand, pulling her along through the guests as they made their way out a side door that would take them toward the back of the house and near the servant's stairs.

Instead of going up the stairs, however, Giles turned them down a small passage. He moved them toward the conservatory and one of Sarah's favorite places at the estate.

The smell of summer bombarded her senses, roses and foliage of earth along with the trickle of water from the large, circular fountain.

The room was warmer than other parts of the house, as it had a constant source of heat from the two large fires that burned beside the wide glass doors leading into the room during winter.

Giles shut the doors, the snip of the lock echoing about the space.

Sarah turned and watched as he gestured to the space. "The first night that you kissed me in London was warm, and although we cannot sneak outside and kiss against the ivy, I can kiss you properly here, in a room reminiscent of that time."

Her heart lurched, and she went to him, wrapping her arms about his neck. "A new beginning, since you made such a mess of things ten years ago," she teased, chuckling.

Giles growled, hoisting her up against his side. "Kiss me, Sarah, and see if you're rid of me."

Sarah did as he asked, and finally, the marquess was hers, and in no way would she lose him again.

"Merry Christmas, my love," he said, pulling but a breath away from her.

Tears welled in her eyes at how happy she was. How happy he made her feel. "Merry Christmas."

Thank you for taking the time to read *The Marquess is Mine*! I hope you enjoyed the sixth book in my League of Unweddable Gentlemen series.

I adore my readers, and I'm so thankful for your support with my books. If you're able, I would appreciate an honest review of *The Marquess is Mine*. As they say, feed an author, leave a review!

If you'd like to learn about book one in my Royal House of Atharia series, *To Dream of You*, please read on. I have included chapter one for your reading pleasure.

Tamara Gill

TO DREAM OF YOU

THE ROYAL HOUSE OF ATHARIA, BOOK 1

After months spent in hiding, Princess Holly is finally ready to take her rightful place as ruler of Atharia. All she has to do now is survive her murderous uncle's attempts to steal the throne for himself. But when a mysterious gentleman washes up on the shores of her beach, she's shocked to realize she needs his help almost as much as he needs hers …

. . .

When Drew Meyers left his estate, his plan was to escape the arranged marriage, his scheming father brokered for him. The storm that nearly killed him was not part of the plan. Neither was meeting her. Holly is everything he ever wanted, and he will do anything to keep her safe and get her home—even if doing so means he'll be forced to let her go forever…

A union between a princess and a lowly future duke is forbidden. But as intrigue abounds and their enemies circle, will Drew and Holly defy the obligations and expectations that stand between them to take a chance on love? Or is their happily ever after merely a dream?

CHAPTER 1

Sotherton Estate, Suffolk, 1805

My Lord Balhannah,
Drew…
I write to you today from necessity and desperation, and I hope you shall heed my words and help me due to our friendship. There is no doubt in my mind that in the coming days your father shall demand that our marriage takes place forthwith. In fact, as I write this, my father is readying the coaches to travel two days hence. I assume a marriage license has already been procured and contracts signed, unbeknown to us of course…until today.
Know that as much as I admire and care for you as a friend, I do not love, nor do I wish to marry you, as I'm sure you do not want to marry me. You see, my heart has long been given elsewhere, and I will not, not even on pain of disinheritance, give up the man I love.
When we arrive at Sotherton, please do not be there, unless you wish to break my heart and give yourself to me before God, when you know that I shall never love you how a wife should love a husband. If you can provide me with time, my love has promised to come and collect me at Sotherton, where we shall run away to Scotland and be

married. I'm sorry to be so frank with my words, but I'm desperate to get this letter to you and, with it, stress how much I do not want such a union.
Please do whatever you can to dissuade this marriage from going ahead.
Forever your friend,
Myrtle

Drew placed the missive from Myrtle into the fire in his room and went to the window. He pulled back the heavy brocade velvet curtains to gauge the weather. A perfect spring day, and from his window, he could see the sea and the cove where his small sailing raft was kept.

Absently he listened to his valet, Jeffries behind him go about his duties in his room. He could not stay here. Not with Myrtle so heartsick over their impending marriage. With his decision made, he turned and faced his servant. "I'm going sailing and may even travel down the coast to visit Sir Percival's at Castle Clair in Kent. I will meet you there. Please pack me a small bag to get me through until we meet again. Nothing too fancy, mind you, we'll be mostly hunting or taking our leisure about the estate. Maybe only two dinner jackets."

Jeffries stared at him, his eyes wide with this change of plans. Drew raised one brow, waiting for him to comprehend he was serious with his demand.

"Of course, my lord." Jeffries started for the chest of drawers, pulling out cravats and buckskin breeches before walking into Drew's dressing room to collect a trunk. "Will His Grace be aware of your travels, my lord, or are we keeping this excursion a secret?" Jeffries asked, from the small room.

Drew went to his chest of drawers and pulled out the oldest buckskin breeches he owned. He stripped his perfectly tied cravat from his throat, along with his waistcoat. Rummaging through his cupboard, he couldn't find his old woolen waistcoat that was warm and what he liked to use for sailing. "I cannot locate my…" Drew smiled when Jeffries passed it to him, a small smile on the man's face. "Thank you," he said, slipping it on, along with his coat.

Drew walked over to his desk and scribbled a short note to his father. Folding it, he handed it to his manservant. "Have this sent from London when you move through there. The duke may travel to town and demand answers, he will try to find me, but he will not succeed. Under no circumstances are you to tell him where I've gone. I will send a word in a week notifying you, God willing, of my safe arrival." His father was ruthless when it came to having his way, the marriage to Myrtle no different. He would lose his allowance, Drew had little doubt, but what of it? It would not be forever. Myrtle would run away and marry, and then Drew could return home.

Thank heavens Miss Landers was also against the union and only needed time to ensure their marriage would never happen. And time is what he was buying now.

Jeffries handed him a small black valise. "Yes, my lord."

Drew pocketed some blunt and left, leaving via the servant's stairs and the back door, two places his father's shadow never darkened. He ran a hand through his short locks, pulling on a cap to disguise himself further.

The brisk, salty tang of sea air hit him and invigorated his stride. Drew walked through the abundance of gardens his mother had so painstakingly cared for before passing last year. Memories of running about the garden bombarded his mind. Of hidden vistas and large oaks that any young boy enjoyed frolicking around whenever he could. His mother had designed the garden to incorporate hidden vistas perfect for children. Plants that camouflaged the old Roman ruins on the south side of the park, so it wasn't until you were almost upon them did the ruins reveal themselves, the long-lost castle of the Sotherton dukes who came before them.

Drew had spent hours playing on his own within the walls of this green sanctuary. As much as he disliked having the idea of a wife at this very moment, he couldn't help but look forward to the day his children would run about the beautiful grounds and enjoy what he always had.

The crashing of the waves echoed through the trees. Stepping free of the manicured grounds, Drew stood at the top of the small cliff and looked down on the beach's golden sands below. Many years ago, he'd had a small boathouse built to house his sailboat, and as the tide was high, it would be no problem pulling it out and dragging it the short distance to the water.

Taking the winding path down to the shore, it didn't take him long to haul the boat into the shallows and throw his bag under the little compartment that would keep it dry. The sky remained clear, with only the slightest sea breeze. It would help him travel down the coast to where his friend and closest confidant Sir Percival lived. The trip should only take a few days, and he couldn't get far enough away from this estate. To be forced into a union, not of his choice, or Miss Lander's, was reprehensible. The year was 1805, for heaven's sake. His father really ought to get up with the times. Step into the nineteenth century and embrace the new era. He was a grown gentleman, fully capable of making his own decisions. For his father to demand he marry, simply because he'd stumbled across an heiress, was offensive.

Drew pushed off from the shore, releasing the sail. The wind caught the sheet and pulled him out to sea at a clipping pace. He steered south and smiled. His father would forgive him in time, he was sure of it. The duke was never one to hold a grudge for long, and no matter how mad he'd be at finding out Drew left, he would get over it in time.

LORDS OF LONDON SERIES AVAILABLE NOW!

Dive into these charming historical romances! In this six-book series, Darcy seduces a virginal duke, Cecilia's world collides with a roguish marquess, Katherine strikes a deal with an unlucky earl and Lizzy sets out to conquer a very wicked Viscount. These stories plus more adventures in the Lords of London series! Available now through Amazon or read free with KindleUnlimited.

KISS THE WALLFLOWER SERIES AVAILABLE NOW!

If the roguish Lords of London are not for you and wallflowers are more your cup of tea, this is the series for you. My Kiss the Wallflower series, are linked through friendship and family in this four-book series. You can grab a copy on Amazon or read free through KindleUnlimited.

THE ROYAL HOUSE OF ATHARIA SERIES

If you love dashing dukes and want a royal adventure, make sure to check out my latest series, The Royal House of Atharia series! Book one, To Dream of You is available now at Amazon or you can read FREE with Kindle Unlimited.

A union between a princess and a lowly future duke is forbidden. But as intrigue abounds and their enemies circle, will Drew and Holly defy the obligations and expectations that stand between them to take a chance on love? Or is their happily ever after merely a dream?

ALSO BY TAMARA GILL

Royal House of Atharia Series

TO DREAM OF YOU

A ROYAL PROPOSITION

FOREVER MY PRINCESS

ROYAL ATHARIA - BOOKS 1-3 BUNDLE

League of Unweddable Gentlemen Series

TEMPT ME, YOUR GRACE

HELLION AT HEART

DARE TO BE SCANDALOUS

TO BE WICKED WITH YOU

KISS ME DUKE

THE MARQUESS IS MINE

LEAGUE - BOOKS 1-3 BUNDLE

LEAGUE - BOOKS 4-6 BUNDLE

Kiss the Wallflower series

A MIDSUMMER KISS

A KISS AT MISTLETOE

A KISS IN SPRING

TO FALL FOR A KISS

A DUKE'S WILD KISS

TO KISS A HIGHLAND ROSE

KISS THE WALLFLOWER - BOOKS 1-3 BUNDLE

KISS THE WALLFLOWER - BOOKS 4-6 BUNDLE

Lords of London Series

TO BEDEVIL A DUKE

TO MADDEN A MARQUESS

TO TEMPT AN EARL

TO VEX A VISCOUNT

TO DARE A DUCHESS

TO MARRY A MARCHIONESS

LORDS OF LONDON - BOOKS 1-3 BUNDLE

LORDS OF LONDON - BOOKS 4-6 BUNDLE

To Marry a Rogue Series

ONLY AN EARL WILL DO

ONLY A DUKE WILL DO

ONLY A VISCOUNT WILL DO

ONLY A MARQUESS WILL DO

ONLY A LADY WILL DO

TO MARRY A ROGUE - BOOKS 1-5 BUNDLE

A Time Traveler's Highland Love Series

TO CONQUER A SCOT

TO SAVE A SAVAGE SCOT

TO WIN A HIGHLAND SCOT

HIGHLAND LOVE - BOOKS 1-3 BUNDLE

A Stolen Season Series

A STOLEN SEASON

A STOLEN SEASON: BATH

A STOLEN SEASON: LONDON

Time Travel Romance

DEFIANT SURRENDER

Scandalous London Series

A GENTLEMAN'S PROMISE

A CAPTAIN'S ORDER

A MARRIAGE MADE IN MAYFAIR

SCANDALOUS LONDON - BOOKS 1-3 BUNDLE

High Seas & High Stakes Series

HIS LADY SMUGGLER

HER GENTLEMAN PIRATE

HIGH SEAS & HIGH STAKES - BOOKS 1-2 BUNDLE

Daughters Of The Gods Series

BANISHED-GUARDIAN-FALLEN

DAUGHTERS OF THE GODS - BOOKS 1-3 BUNDLE

Stand Alone Books

TO SIN WITH SCANDAL

OUTLAWS

ABOUT THE AUTHOR

Tamara is an Australian author who grew up in an old mining town in country South Australia, where her love of history was founded. So much so, she made her darling husband travel to the UK for their honeymoon, where she dragged him from one historical monument and castle to another.

A mother of three, her two little gentlemen in the making, a future lady (she hopes) and a part-time job keep her busy in the real world, but whenever she gets a moment's peace she loves to write romance novels in an array of genres, including regency, medieval and time travel.

www.tamaragill.com
tamaragillauthor@gmail.com

Made in the USA
Columbia, SC
02 June 2022